Anomie

Anomie

Everything, Volume One

STEVEN DELAY

RESOURCE *Publications* · Eugene, Oregon

ANOMIE
Everything, Volume One

Resource Publications
An Imprint of Wipf and Stock Publishers
199 W. 8th Ave., Suite 3
Eugene, OR 97401

www.wipfandstock.com

PAPERBACK ISBN: 978-1-6667-3831-5
HARDCOVER ISBN: 978-1-6667-9884-5
EBOOK ISBN: 978-1-6667-9885-2

APRIL 25, 2022 12:04 PM

As always,
to Gabriella

"And it shall come to pass in the day that the Lord shall give thee rest from thy sorrow, and from thy fear, and from the hard bondage wherein thou was made to serve.

That thou shalt take up this proverb against the king of Babylon, and say, How hath the oppressor ceased! The golden city ceased!

The Lord hath broken the staff of the wicked, and the sceptre of the rulers."

ISAIAH 14:3–5

ONE

I T would be easy. Nothing to it, really. "Meet me there at seven," it said. Toying the text over, he had spent the early afternoon hours smoking cigarettes in his apartment living room, debating whether or not he should show up early later that evening. It was Tuesday, so if the usual bartender was working, he might get a free shot of Fireball. Whiskey always made him gag a little, and if things went well, he would have to be careful not to get too drunk as the night drew on, but in this case, one quick shot tonight might be worth the risk, since it would settle his nerves, and help him feel natural.

He told himself that, in any event, he had to remember there was always the fact that even if nothing happened tonight, things would probably go well enough to mean it would that weekend. The thought helped ease the self-consciousness over his sweaty palms. He hated when they got like this. He kept wiping them on his shirt on the walk over to the bar, but to no avail. Still clammy. When they went to greet each other with a hug tonight, he thought, she could of course decide to believe it was only the summer humidity. But it was a longshot, he knew. She would know he was anxious. Maybe she would find that cute or flattering. The whole thing was nothing to think about anyway, he finally decided, just something he was worrying over for no good reason. People's hands get sweaty sometimes. Even hers. Everyone knows that. Silly to lend it any more thought than he already had.

He climbed the stairs to the door, rolled up the shirt sleeves to his elbows, peeled off the fabric from sticking against his side, and then walked through the entrance. "Hey man," the bartender said, as he stepped in.

Blinded from the bright sun outside, he made his way through the dim interior. He sat down on a stool at the counter's elbow, and glanced out the wide front window onto the residential street outside, as he waited for his sight to adjust. In the middle of the park stood the fountain's water sculpture. The figure, Hermes, he assumed, though he had never bothered to read the plaque's inscription, was attracting the sparrows and pigeons. A homeless man was sleeping on a bench in the shade. In the window's reflection, he noticed the bartender walking from the ice machine towards him with a napkin for his glass. The bartender placed it on the counter. "How's it going? Shot?" the man asked.

Turning to face the bartender, he cracked a sheepish smile. "Sure."

He wondered whether the bartender knew he was sad, wondered whether the bartender himself was sad too, wondered whether the bartender wondered whether he ever wondered whether they, like everyone else, were both sad. Sometimes in life there didn't seem to be any point in saying what really matters, since it didn't stand to change anything. He thought about how words are strange like that. Sometimes they can do something. Other times they can't. What was the point in stating that something just is the way it is? Words don't alter or improve anything about it. The situation makes speaking redundant. Emotions, desires, thoughts, even events themselves—they are like animals at the zoo. Items at which we just look and point. And still, despite feeling the futility of his words to accomplish anything worthwhile, as he watched the whiskey pour into the glass, he found himself imagining what would happen if he did tell the bartender what was on his mind. He felt a rush of exhilaration at the possibility, but before he could continue playing with the scenario, it evaporated, the flight of fancy dispelled by the realization that his tongue, as if possessed by a mind of its own, was already in motion. "Thanks," he heard himself say.

They nodded glumly to each other, clinked glasses, and both swigged back the burn.

"Let me know if you want another one," the bartender said.

Two others were sitting silently next to one another at the other end of the counter, coworkers by the looks of it, and they glanced up from their phones as the bartender went to serve them. Shouldn't have done that shot, he thought to himself. He sighed softly. His gaze drifted across the crimson wall behind the bar, and found the tilted clock hanging above the refrigerated beer. The time read five-thirty. Well, now he knew he will have already had two or three shots by the time it was seven. The amusing Pascal line that routinely had been coming to mind flashed again into his consciousness, "All of mankind's problems stem . . . "

ONE

"Could you turn that up?" one of the men at the counter asked the bartender.

The bartender walked over to the stereo system, and turned the knob.

"You like Chet Baker?" the bartender asked.

"Is that who this is?" the second man at the counter said.

"Yeah, it's a mix. Baker, Coltrane, Billie Holiday," the bartender said.

This was a mood he'd experienced before, he thought, one where all things feel like they were a game. That life itself was an experiment, but without any right answer. As a child in elementary school, especially during the closing weeks of the school year approaching summer vacation, he had sometimes been struck by the contingency of it all, that he was at this school rather than some other, that he was in this grade rather than the one above him, that he lived where he did rather than in Massachusetts or some other distant place he'd heard of or had read about in a book. His teacher, Ms. Kearley, he could see, was in a way a child just like them, only in a bigger body. Everyone he knew was there without knowing how or why. But nobody ever said it. When he had wondered at the time whether the adults recognized it, and simply chose not to say so, because they understood the children would one day figure it out on their own eventually, he would stare out the classroom window onto the play yard's trees and tables, temporarily released from the boredom, consoled by the thought that, if everything were in fact a big game, then none of what his teacher or anyone else said really mattered. Maybe everyone was wrong about everything. How would they know? When, then, she would tell them all, "Live and Let Live," he felt as if his teacher's mantra were a feeble attempt at answering a deeper question she would not raise explicitly. He had heard stories from his father about how, in the past, the entire Valley would have at that time of year been abloom with apricot and plum orchards for as far as the eye could see. Eventually had come the defense firms and with it the suburban sprawl, and then in turn the technology companies, which only made the congestion worse. When he was born, by then all of the orchards had already disappeared, and what used to be was gone. He would stare out the school window trying to imagine the past to his surroundings he had never known, and would think about how one day he and all his friends and everyone they knew would all be gone, too.

Now, sitting at the bar as a young man at that stage in his twenties when thirty still feels remote, he realized that everything had only proved to confirm what he had suspected while daydreaming as a child. Just as the

3

school's name, Old Orchard, was a testament to one irretrievable past of Bay Area history, so too it was a reminder that the current present here in Texas would in the future likewise fade away, forgotten like every other past that had preceded it. Everything was forgetting. The recognition that everything he knew now was destined to disappear didn't fill him with dread, as many of the philosophers he read all said that it should, but it did make him sad. Truth be told, sometimes he resented others who tried pretending as if they sincerely liked it this way, as if they weren't really bothered by the fleetingness haunting everything that they claimed to hold so dear. As far as he could tell, either they must not truly love what they say they love as much as they say they do, or else they must be hiding the sadness of knowing things are a vapor, he thought. At some point, he presumed, like him they had also discovered that perhaps life was nothing more than an experiment, and that nobody really knew what to do with existence. It was a notion that seemed to him obvious and inescapable, yet something about the idea of existence merely being an experiment could never sit well with him. Those words from the lips of the one who imbibed the spirit of Zarathustra came to mind, "Hearing the news . . . we philosophers and free spirits feel illuminated by a new dawn; our heart overflows with gratitude, amazement, forebodings, expectation . . . " He didn't deny that many people he had met appeared to relish the spirit of Nietzsche's proclamation, as if a heavy weight had finally been lifted off their shoulders, and they could at last relax after admitting to themselves that nothing really mattered. For his own part, though, he found such an attitude to life's transience unnerving. There was something repulsive about seeing others deciding that, because time leads to death, existence for them would be about bodily pleasure, or egoistic gratification, or social success, or whatever other transient thing they wanted to seek comfort in. It all seemed too easy, too self-serving. Of course, as he would be the first to acknowledge, he himself ultimately was no exception, sitting as he was here at the bar. But at least he was honest about it all, he thought.

He took a sip of his beer, and walked out onto the downstairs patio, where he lit a cigarette. He exhaled, and stared at the smoke rising to the ceiling. Then again, he thought, because nobody really talked about so much of what makes life what it is, he was left to concede that maybe others felt exactly the same way he did. For all he knew, maybe they assumed they were the only ones who had such insights, while it was all the others, himself included, who were oblivious to the reality of existence's being a game.

Five university students walked up the entryway stairs, laughing with each other as the bearded doorman checked their IDs. Yes, in looking on, he saw how, to them, he must be just another faceless somebody who didn't know what they took themselves alone to know. But if everyone's the same, stuck playing this game, then invariably these students must have at some point had his same thoughts, meaning they too had realized that, in the eyes of others, it was they who would appear to be the clueless ones bumbling through life oblivious to their own obliviousness. But, then, if that were the case, then—he felt his mind beginning to spin. He would file the thought away for the time being, to revisit it later, to think his way down to the bottom of wherever the spiraling vortex of logic might take him. At the moment, he wasn't in the mood for hyper-reflection. In the final analysis, there was no end to it anyway. Eventually, even the act of thinking is itself seen to be pointless, he had concluded many times before. Camus's absurdity, right? Shaking his head, he chuckled to himself. Why, he wondered, did people always attach another's name to their own thoughts? A thought's a thought. It suddenly seemed so odd to him how even within the privacy of his own mind he could succumb so easily to the temptation, to the rule that he must attribute his thoughts to somebody else. He wondered if others did that too. He looked at the park fountain across the street, finished his beer with a gulp, took a final drag on his cigarette, left the empty can on the patio's railing overhanging the sidewalk, leaned out to stick his face into the shining sun, and then walked back in.

Inside, the bartender was wiping down the glasses stacked next to the refrigerator. The bartender turned his head to glance over his shoulder. He raised his hand in order to get the bartender's attention. "A Lone Star and another whiskey, please, Billy," he said. He stared out into the space illuminated softly by the red bordello lamps and chandeliers. It was an oddity that had struck him before, and which he could not explain, that somehow even in the midst of an existence he knew technically may not have mattered, good manners nonetheless retained their charm.

Two

I
F everything's an illusion, then nothing is. That, he thought, would
be the first premise in any argument that stood a plausible chance of
refuting nihilism. After all, in order to draw any legitimate distinction
between mere appearance and reality, there must be something genuinely
real. But, so the line of thought would continue, to insist that everything is
illusion is to abolish the distinction between reality and appearance, and
that means the very notion of appearance, and hence illusion itself as well,
would slip into incoherence. *Ergo*, because it entails the elimination of the
distinction between appearance and reality, nihilism, which thereby implies
everything is an illusion, must be false. That seemed right. He was sure,
though, that if he were to write it down on paper and think it over more
carefully, he would find something about it that somebody would allege
to be a flaw in its reasoning. And, anyway, even if it were flawless, anyone
who didn't want to accept the conclusion that nihilism is false would be
required to object to it, nevertheless. At that point, naturally he could argue
that the very act of objecting to the argument in question is a performative
contradiction, since somebody's arguing that there is no point to anything
itself presupposes there at least is a point to arguing so. In response, the
self-proclaimed nihilist would introduce some subtlety to avoid the charge
of self-refutation, probably by arguing that the claim of self-stultification
was equivocating on the meaning of the word "point." Thus, so on and so
forth it would continue. It was all precisely as Fichte had said, "What sort
of philosophy one chooses depends on..." The entire argument he was currently imagining, and which he had actually participated in many times
before, felt empty to him in a way that made him wonder how different he

was from the nihilist. If having the argument wasn't worth having, was the nihilist really wrong?

Were he here, his friend David Itlas, for instance, no doubt would begin by magnanimously conceding that the argument was certainly clever, and then proceed to attempt to shred it. He thought about giving David a call, to see whether he and his roommate Jack Murphy wanted to come for a beer, but that would only unnecessarily perturb everyone. David was the type who had struggled from youth with attracting girls, and his girlfriend Margo, or rather now ex-girlfriend, who had been living in New York City, had left him recently. Given the rawness of the break-up, and his tendency to view the actions of others as underhanded attempts to slight him, David would predictably interpret an invitation tonight to the bar as an obvious ploy to flaunt the fact that he was meeting a girl, whereas David was not. It was the petty kind of behavior from David that he usually could overlook. Ever since moving to Houston a few years ago, he'd grown accustomed to facing whatever judgment David's inferiority complex was bound to elicit. He had done so for the sake of the philosophical discussion. David's surliness had come with the territory, and it had seemed worthwhile. For one thing, their mutual friends appreciated David's wit and humor, and because their friend's bespectacled face and disheveled hair was a permanent fixture at all the house parties, he was impossible to avoid. It only made sense to try to focus on his endearing qualities, rather than to dwell on what made him irritating. Lately, however, he had been growing tired of the intellectual sparring, not just David's snide comments and innuendos. So, tonight would be as good as any other to try something different. He put his phone back in his pocket, and went back to waiting for seven.

A chubby, balding businessman in a frumpy brown suit entered and took a seat at one of the booths at the front window. He began looking at the menu. Occasionally he would peer out the window, evidently waiting on someone who was supposed to be joining him. A few minutes later, another man came through the door and strode up to the booth, took a seat, removed his suit jacket and loosened his periwinkle tie, and grabbed a menu. After placing their food orders with the woman working at the kitchen, the two walked to the bar counter, took their drinks, and then sat down again, where they sat while pointing and laughing at what they were watching on the television. At the moment, the television was turned to some cable sports channel, and later in the evening, as was the custom, it would be playing old black and white Hollywood movies. The procession of patrons steadily increased, as more customers filed into the bar. By about six-thirty, there wasn't a seat left at the counter or the booths, and the front patio where he had smoked his cigarette was full also, which meant people were beginning to trickle up to the upstairs balcony. This was unusually busy for a Tuesday.

He asked the man next to him to watch his seat, and he walked down the black and white striped hallway connecting the bar to the restrooms. He splashed his face with some water and dried his hands with a paper towel. As he returned to the counter staring at his feet, he mulled over whether the hallway's chess board theme was just an innocent decorating decision, or whether the bar's owner had meant to signal by it a Freemasonic connection. Those initiated into that world, especially business types, delighted in making it clear to others in the know, because it was good for business. For a start, it helped garner leniency with the law. The underworld's presence couldn't be overlooked anywhere, certainly not in here. The brothel operating two blocks away in broad daylight, for instance, was an open secret to everyone in the neighborhood, and apparently there were even a number of police officers who regularly frequented it. In all likelihood, much of the drug-dealing that occurred at the bar, and at other places like it in the area, was known to the police, but so long as the police got their cut, none of the employees, or policeman, or anyone else, would ever say a word. He remembered an old friend of his whose brother was an inventor and small business owner, once telling him about the existence of corporate espionage and blackmail. His friend's brother's company had been ripped off by a large corporation that stole the brother's product. When the CEO of the company responsible for the theft died in a private plane crash a few years later, his friend couldn't help but laugh, since as far as he was concerned, the man had what was coming to him. He had come home one afternoon to find his friend standing alone on the back porch in the garden smoking a cigarette in the sun, a grin on his face.

"What happened?" he asked.

"Klein died yesterday. Plane crash," his friend had answered.

He finally had crossed the wrong powerful competitor, and that had been it for him, his friend said. When the next year his old friend began complaining about neurological ailments that he suspected were the result from a night in which he had been poisoned at a Chinese restaurant in Portland, their other roommates stopped taking seriously his friend's stories about the criminal underworld. They dismissed him as paranoid. But he always felt like there was a core of insight in them, even now.

Take the two men eating together in the booth. The second one to enter, who was Chinese, could be a perfectly innocuous energy executive, or accountant, or partner at a legal firm. But how did anyone know for certain? The Chinese Consulate was just down the street from the bar, and if the Chinese Communist Party had hired him to gather information from the other man at the booth, the latter likely would be none the wiser. And if the man slipped something into the other man's drink that killed him, like his old friend had claimed somebody had tried in Portland, who would know? Somebody might note that one could always go to the police, but what good would that do, when the police themselves were the ones protecting much of the crime, like at the brothel? For his own part, at any rate, he always tried to ignore the drugs at the bar. Not out of a fear of being poisoned, but moral sensitivity. As much as he drank and smoked, drugs made him uncomfortable. It had always seemed to him that using drugs was a way of admitting that one had finally quit, and so he felt a mix of pity and aversion for those who did them.

At the counter, the man he had asked to hold his seat had left, and the seat had been taken, but another one had opened up, so he sat down there instead and called Billy.

"Whiskey and Lone Star, please," he said.

By the time it reached the point in the night when he realized that the bar would be closing soon, he complimented himself for not having thought about it since around ten o'clock. Rebecca hadn't shown up, which wasn't entirely unexpected, since, if he now were being honest, she had appeared to be the type who enjoyed appearing busier than she was, and although he was a little embarrassed that she hadn't come or even contacted him to explain why not, he decided there was comfort in being alone at the moment, perched at the bar like a Nighthawk, able to watch others, to surmise what they did, where they were from, and what they thought was giving their night purpose. A friend of Rebecca's was there in the downstairs crowd, talking to others. She had arrived at midnight, and had not looked over once at him, but he assumed she would tell Rebecca that she had seen him there alone. She and her companions nudged their way through the crowd to the bar, ordered another round, then headed up the stairs. He noticed that she looked at him right before disappearing from view. She probably was hoping to judge whether he was there waiting. He thought it was funny, that even at their age things had not changed much from the dynamics of middle school. If Rebecca and her friends thought that he was sculpting a style that he wanted them to see, they were wrong. He didn't care. Or at least he was rather sure he didn't care. How could anyone, including himself, really know with certainty? What's the standard by which one could decide such things, anyway? Probably Wittgenstein had something enlightening to say about the situation, but he had never read any Wittgenstein, though the name arose constantly in conversations among his university friends. In the immediate aftermath of her not showing up, he had guzzled a few beers in rapid succession, which had left him lethargic for an hour or so, but as the night unfolded, he ended up feeling fairly alert, and relatively placid, all things considered. He was still restless in that way he always was, with that longing feeling that there was somewhere better to be, only to have the realization moments later that there wasn't anywhere else to be, that this was where he was, and that was just the way it is. Maybe she and her friends wanted to see how he would react to the situation, but instead of calling or texting her to play along, or heading upstairs to talk to her little envoy, he decided he was done with it.

Somebody standing behind him kept elbowing him in the back. Although sitting at the bar was convenient because it meant he didn't have to stand, there was somebody continually squeezing into the little spaces to his either side to order. He liked listening to what they wanted, and sometimes he would try to guess what they would ask for before they did. Just as he was preparing to leave, Billy came over and asked if he would like a final round before it was time to close out. On nights like these when it could take ten or fifteen minutes to get one's turn, it was nice to have the bartender come to him. There was no reason to feel proud about it, of course. Being a regular at the bar wasn't anything to boast about, but in the frenzy of emotions and the swirl of voices and intermingled bodies, there was something satisfying about it. On nights like these, very often people would ask whether he might order for them, but he would say no, since he assumed one of the reasons Billy continued to let him cut the line was because he didn't abuse his privilege.

"Lemon Drop, please."

"A shot of it?"

"Yes, a shot, not a cocktail." He forgot to say please.

As Billy was mixing the shot, a couple nudged in beside him. The man was in his twenties, with styled black hair, a gold watch, and a button-down and jacket. He was tall, well over six feet, with a tan complexion that suggested he was Italian, maybe middle-eastern.

The girl turned from her companion and looked at him, "What are you having?"

At first, he was confused. They had never met. Maybe she was talking to someone sitting behind him, he thought, or had simply mistaken him for somebody she knew.

"Uh, a Lemon Drop," he said, pointing awkwardly to Billy.

"I love those," she said.

The man she was with turned to Billy, "Two more Lemon Drops, then."

From the way they talked to Billy, it was clear Billy knew the two as well as he knew Billy, but he had never seen them there before. He would have remembered seeing her. Billy lined out the shots, including one for himself. They all grabbed one, looked at each other and laughed, and drank down the juicy concoction. The girl was beautiful, with big searching brown eyes, black hair, and porcelain skin. He couldn't remember the last time a girl had intimidated him, but he was scared to talk to her, afraid that he would say something stupid. He could tell she was smart. Despite her sensuality, there was a purity to it, as if she were a saint passing through this place to which she didn't belong, to encourage everyone else there that they were out of place, too, if only they would remember it, and recall who they had once been before they'd become what they were now. The man she was with was probably her boyfriend, although it was ambiguous, because the man, judging by his effeminate mannerisms, could just as well been homosexual. Before he had any further opportunity to wonder, the man wrapped his arm around her, kissed her, and the two laughed. He could feel himself receding from her awareness, her attention drawn to others at the counter, and he knew it would look pathetic to say anything. Without ever deciding to do so, he found himself tapping her on the shoulder. Mortified at himself, he relaxed when she spun around, a pleasant smile on her face. He told her his name.

"I'm Alison," she said.

They shook hands, a gesture that was overly formal, comic really, given the circumstances, but so it was. The man she was with turned to them both, and without a hint of jealousy, introduced himself as well.

"Justice," he said, extending his hand.

There were the girls he had met named after the theological virtues—Hope, Faith, Charity—but this was the first time he'd ever met a man named after a virtue. He chuckled to himself, took it as a sign that he ought not to meddle, closed out his tab, and left without saying another word to the couple, or to anyone else.

He strode down the stairs to the sidewalk, brushing past the groups of people congregating outside while chatting and smoking in the muggy night. A few girls smiled at him, but he ignored them, because he was still thinking about the couple from inside. Headlights from the idling cars flooded the street, as their passengers readied to leave for whatever after parties were being planned. A few cyclists whizzed past. He glanced behind the taco truck to make sure the coast was clear of traffic, and he crossed the street. He heard the raucousness from the balcony, the sound of laughter and shouting over the music. He turned back to look. The white Christmas lights they kept up all year round were dangling from the upstairs walls, and the downstairs red interior light, which sometimes looked sinister, appeared almost homey. After a few minutes of watching, he turned away to walk home, passing the park fountain and Hermes along the way. The man who had been sleeping on the bench was nowhere to be seen, and the birds were tucked away in their nests. A strong wind blew through the big oaks, and the cicadas suddenly quieted down. A block from home, there was a loud clap of thunder, and moments later a torrential rain started pouring. He didn't feel like running, so he lifted his face upward to the night sky, opened his mouth, and felt the droplets strike his neck and face. When he reached the building's front garden, its wet grass and shrubs were glistening in the moonlight, the rain pelting like gunfire against the hoods of the parked cars on the street.

Inside in the hall, he could hear his neighbor down the way in the corner unit was still up. Its tenant, Timothy Mangs, was a medical student. He was brilliant, and kind too. But lately the pressure and drudgery of the medical rounds was beginning to tax him, and as his dependence on marijuana and hallucinogens to relax had worsened, he was becoming noticeably erratic. Timothy would talk uninterruptedly for long stretches, and when one finally had the chance to respond, he wouldn't hear a word before launching in again into another spiel. His long white blond hair and fiery blue eyes had always given him the look of a Nordic warrior, but now there was something unsettling about his neighbor's inner ferocity. His thoughts would come in barrages, sometimes bordering on the incoherent, almost as if he were narrating aloud his subconscious, just to see how others would react or how long they could endure it.

Two

Timothy, in a word, was someone who was also recognizing that so much of everyday life is pretense, that there is very little reason for what most people say or do, and that much of social life is tolerating the inanity of it all. When it came down to it, his neighbor couldn't reconcile his true motivations for being at medical school with the norms of the profession. He would complain about how his fellow medical students had no desire to truly understand medicine, but only cared about learning what they had to learn for their exams. As for the doctors themselves, many of them were arrogant and self-centered, more concerned with impressing their colleagues than they were serving the sick. To cope, his neighbor had been steadily freeing himself from the bonds of social expectation, including the norms at the hospital. Clearly, it was giving him a thrill, and it only reinforced the underlying conviction spurring it, that everything was all just theater anyway. He didn't fault Timothy for regarding much of everydayness as purely groundless, and sometimes he couldn't help but laugh at the amusing stories his neighbor told him about how he was finding some new way of subverting the silly protocol of doing things in his program, but he did worry that his neighbor's volatile experiment in nonconformism was taking a detrimental turn. At the very least, there was too much self-indulgence in it all. When he would ask Timothy whether he was truly prepared to flunk out, his neighbor would say yes, but he noticed that Timothy would invariably mention how he didn't care if his parents, both of whom were psychiatrists, would mind if he never finished medical school. It was difficult not to conclude that his parents had probably placed considerable pressure on him to follow the path of medicine, and maybe this was his way of finally saying no to it. Timothy's sister, Tanya, who was from another city, San Antonio if memory served, had been to visit a few weeks ago, probably to try to keep the family peace. At work, of course, nobody saw Timothy as a rebellious son or difficult brother who was defying his demanding parents and worrying his responsible sister. In a way, the fact that nobody knew it, only underscored his gripe about how modern work life, even in the medical field, was superficial, a place where one did what one was expected to do, and that was it.

The music from Timothy's apartment blared through the walls, echoing through the hall. If his neighbor had not passed out and was still awake, at this hour that would mean he was stoned and manic. He knew that he would have to talk to Timothy the next time they saw each other, to make sure he was holding up. But as for now, rather than knock on his door and walk into what would be too overwhelming of a situation, he instead walked straight to his own door, turned the key, and stepped inside. For a brief moment, he was flooded by an overwhelming feeling of melancholy, of how broken everyone he knew was. He threw his soaking clothes in a pile on the floor, flopped down on the bed, and went to sleep.

THREE

T HE next day, he woke up late. He washed some dishes that had been lying in the kitchen sink for too long. Some of the spaghetti sauce from the pan splattered on his shirt, but he didn't bother changing it. Then he sat down on the discolored white couch in the living room. The chances of anything happening the rest of the week were remote, he felt. He didn't know what the absence of expectation was even precisely directed toward, but it was there. If nothing else, he thought, there were always books, so he took one from the shelf next to the door and began reading.

Saturday came. It was Mick Firth's twenty-eighth birthday. When he got to the house that was rented by their mutual friends, Paul and Clara, he walked down the gravel driveway, following the sound of the Aussie's voice booming from the backyard. He turned the corner of the house to find Mick sitting in the grass on a purple beach chair, a Foster's in one hand resting on his lap, the other hand rubbing his fat belly that was shaking from all the laughing. Tony and Cody, two others from the crew, were sitting with Mick and looked up.

"Hey man," Tony said.

"Hi, Tony," he waved. "Happy birthday, Mick."

Mick's blond crew cut was freshly trimmed. He had purchased a new pair of expensive designer black arthouse glasses, the sort somebody else might call hip, though it was a term he himself wouldn't use to describe them, since he had never liked the word. The make-over wasn't timed only for the birthday. Mick, he knew, would be finishing his doctoral work soon, and when he did, it would be time for a professorship somewhere, maybe in his native Australia. That meant it was necessary to start looking the part of university professor, by cleaning up a little.

"Thanks, mate," Mick drawled.

Cody was silent, so he simply nodded. Cody pretended not to see him. To be expected, he thought. He and Cody had never gotten along. It had been something of a competition between them ever since meeting, first over girls, to an extent, then over ideas. Cody was in his twenties, with a bit of premature gray in his beard. He was average height with a somewhat oafish body accentuated by a pair of splay feet, but his piercing blue eyes could be halting, which he had learned how to use to his advantage, by saying a lot with them. He was a smart, ambitious master's philosophy student, with an interest in the philosophy of science, who had set his sights on entering a top doctoral program, meaning he did not expect to be here long, an expectation which tinged his aloof demeanor with a subtext of self-satisfied superiority. According to Cody, because everything was atoms and the void, he had extremely little patience for philosophical systems that attempted to make room for freedom of the will, or human values, and moral truths. As for God, that was completely out of the question, of course, a useless hypothesis, an embarrassing vestige of a more primitive time when our psychological apparatus had still perhaps required it. In time, though, as he would always say, it was inevitable that evolution would continue to progress, at which point our species would finally free itself entirely of such crass superstitions. The timetable involved was impossible to know, but in the interim we could hope to resist catering to such myths any more than was absolutely necessary. It was a materialist's duty. As he opened a beach chair and placed it on the grass next to Cody and the other two, the rest of that Fichte passage entered his mind, "A philosophical system is not a dead piece of furniture that we can accept or reject as we wish, it is rather a thing animated by the soul of the person who holds it."

Turning his gaze to Mick, his attention remained on Cody. He wondered what it was in a soul that explained how somebody could want to believe that everything said to make human life unique and noble was in fact only illusion. Was a man truly no different than the chair he was holding here in his hand? Was everyone just cells contacting other cells? Tony, a philosophy instructor in his early thirties originally from Miami, happened to agree with Cody's sterile conception of the cosmos. Tony, however, didn't seem to take the same perverse delight in the nihilistic idea that Cody did. Tony's grandparents had come to Florida from Cuba to flee

Castro, and his family had instilled an underlying gregariousness in him that made his philosophical views, which were so clinical, appear only to be a veneer, something which he wore like a set of ill-fitting clothes. And as for David, who no doubt would be over to the house soon as well, as irascible and curmudgeonly as he could be, there was a similar gap between life and thought. The proposition that there was no God, no soul, and no immortality clearly tormented him. He recalled the night David had everyone over to his apartment. Taking a drag off his cigarette, exhaling sorrowfully, and addressing the others in the room, David had mused aloud, "Puh! The idea that we have souls? You can't just set a system of thought into motion with an assumption like that. It's unprovable. Nobody knows! I mean, hell, I don't even know if I have a soul." He remembered how David had said it so self-deprecatingly, with a thicker Canadian accent than usual, as if to concede that he understood modern science had sufficiently persuaded him he was only an animal. But David was still torn, and the grief in his eyes revealed that he hadn't abandoned all hope that there was more to man, to himself.

He could hear a car pull up to the front. A minute later, Jack came grinning around the corner, a Marlboro dangling from his lips, his shoulders, already pink from the noon summer sun, exposed by one of those tank-tops he always wore.

"What's up, guys? Ready to party?"

The screen door swung open behind Jack, and then there was David, who had arrived with him. He skipped down the stairs into the yard, along with the renters, Paul and Clara, all three of them wearing matching big straw hats. Everyone was in good spirits. Mick's birthday would be an occasion to try something new for a change, so rather than sitting around drinking all day in the yard, as would be the routine, the plan was to barbeque out at the lake. It was under an hour by car to Huntsville, so they'd have the whole afternoon, even the evening, if they decided to stay for the sunset and a campfire. Tonight the bar would be swarming with young people from the Heights and Montrose, which meant that, without anyone having to say a word, they knew they would all end up there together after returning from the lake.

A few others they all knew from the neighborhood would be coming to the lake this afternoon also, although they wouldn't be stopping at Paul and Clara's place first. They would meet at the lake.

They put the chairs and coolers in the trunk. As they were about to leave, Karl Roybal, Jack's best friend, arrived on his bike. A beach towel wrapped around his neck, the sunscreen on his face barely rubbed in, san-dals poised to slip off his feet, he was the very embodiment of the eccentric, disheveled academic. Karl had shown the most scholarly promise of anyone there. But his journey through the world of academic philosophy had not been pleasant. Not long before coming here, he had clashed with some of the professors at Harvard's philosophy program that he'd been attending at the time. Tired of the professional gamesmanship, he one day had up and quit. The result was that he had ended up back here in his hometown at the local university's philosophy department, where he had ever since been suffering through a terrible case of writer's block. Generally, he was affable and lighthearted, polite and tender, yet beneath the calm exterior was a fierceness, a caustic edge that surfaced especially when he had been drinking or was discussing somebody whose character he didn't respect. Karl and Timothy, it dawned on him, were very similar in many regards, two immensely gifted men who were both busy convincing themselves that honor and authenticity demanded they fail out of the system. To be honest, it was hard to fault them. Graduate school, it had begun to seem to him as well, was more of a compliance test than an intellectual one. After having floated listlessly through a first year in the program, it was now appearing increasingly likely that Karl would quit again by the end of summer, and wouldn't be back for the fall. It was uncertain what would be next for him if he did quit. Recently, he had begun mentioning Austin, and he thought he had once heard Karl mention that he had a sister there. He couldn't remember anyone ever having asked their friend about his parents. Already in his forties, Karl was older than the rest of them, so for all they knew, his parents were already dead. Or maybe just estranged.

The possibility that his troubled friend might commit suicide had crossed his mind more than once. He didn't like thinking about it, but it was impossible not to consider the possibility. Sometimes Karl had a way of saying things that would make people uneasy. To be sure, although he believed in the absoluteness of human freedom, which is why he disagreed so vehemently with Cody and Tony's materialistic determinism, that didn't prevent him from acknowledging that things could certainly appear as if they were fated, as if people, and here Karl appeared to be an exemplary case, had been forced to reconcile themselves to what everybody else knew would inevitably become of them. From what he could tell, Karl had the downcast appearance of someone struggling to resign himself to the ines-capability of his looming professional failure. As he watched Karl chatting with the others by the car, he saw it was unfair how good men like Karl and Timothy were punished for attempting to do what everyone said was right to do, while those in charge of their programs, and who lived high on the hog, openly betrayed the very values their institutions pretended to represent. A world where gentle spirits like Timothy could be the dean of a medical school or Karl the chair of a philosophy department would be vastly superior to this one. And while they never said so to anyone, it was evident that the inversion of it all was driving them both to despair, leading them closer, as if inexorably, to a threshold beyond which the disgust would be too much for them to bear. They both would soon quit, and perhaps the worst part about it was the knowledge that the ones at their programs responsible for demoralizing them to that point knew it would only be a matter of time, just as Timothy and Karl knew it too.

Although the hazing was nothing as blatant as what Karl was facing from the program, he had himself begun wondering whether his own advisor, Saul Carrell, was trying to get him to quit also. He and Saul had a meeting scheduled for next week at the campus coffee house, one which he was dreading, because they would be discussing his term paper that by then would have a grade. It would be a bad grade, he knew. He felt like things were coming to a head. He nearly mentioned the meeting to the others sitting there, but instead of asking for their opinion about how to handle it, he decided he would forget about Carrell for the rest of the day. Karl probably didn't want to talk about school, either.

Inspecting Karl in the afternoon heat, he decided he was witnessing a premonitory figure of what Timothy himself would be in fifteen years, if Timothy really followed through with his plan to destroy his aspirations beginning with his spot in medical school. He wondered what Timothy and Karl would make of each other, if they ever met. Given all of their mutual friends, odds were that by the end of summer they would, perhaps at the bar tonight after the lake. Would they see their similarity? He thought briefly about Dostoevsky's notion of the double, then dropped it.

With the old yellow BMW loaded, it was time to leave. David and Jack, along with Tony and Cody, walked to the car on the street and drove off. Karl, who standing well over six feet was the tallest, thought it would be funny to take the middle seat. He climbed in deliberately goofily, his cheek resting on his knees pulled to his chin, and laughed. Mick took the left rear seat, and he took the right one. Paul was high, his puffy eyes nearly shut, but he knew Paul was the type who did everything that way, including driving, so there was no point in suggesting somebody else should drive, since it would only make Paul more resolved to do it, anyway.

To be sure, the two in the front made for an odd couple. Paul Krutt was a local collage artist, Clara Bell a jewelry maker. When first meeting him, he had found Paul charming. In time, though, what initially seemed to be Paul's natural quirkiness only proved to be an act to cover over his pain. The camouflage jacket he routinely wore was fitting in a way, as it reinforced the impression that he was a soldier of existence growing fatigued with life. The artist suffered from a terrible drinking problem that often made him sloppy, but the occasional embarrassment it caused was something he had learned to accept, since numbing himself helped him accept the inescapability of certain responsibilities he appeared to prefer to be without. His young teenage daughter from a failed marriage was seldom around. Evidently, she lived with the mother. That may have been partly why Paul and Clara themselves weren't yet married. Although he encouraged the image everyone had of him as a libertine and free-spirit, it was clear he would marry Clara if she were willing. Clara, who was the one averse to marriage, or at least to marriage with Paul, allowed others to form the impression that it must be Paul, rather than her, who was the one with cold feet. In any case, he was sure he remembered Paul and Clara having once told everyone why exactly they weren't married, and what their reasons were. Clara had said something about marriage being unnecessary, a point to which everyone at the table had nodded approvingly, but he couldn't quite remember the details of what they all said, because he had been drunk and not paying close attention.

They weaved through the surface streets, and before long, the car was on the highway. They sped across an overpass spanning a stretch of the city's downtown skyline, passing by the baseball stadium. Before the highway returned to ground level, he imagined the car curving along the road from above, as if he were trailing from a helicopter.

As they drove on, he stared up at the blue sky and white clouds. The sun's rays were shining through, casting a magnificent halo down upon the open road. He thought back to when as kids he and his friends would try spotting figures and faces and other things in the clouds. He knew that nobody in the car would want to do that now, unless of course it were to look for dirty things just as a joke. If they played the game, it wouldn't take long for somebody to lodge a point about the human species' penchant for anthropomorphism in religious matters. Our interaction with the natural environment, David would intone were he in the car, is no exception. There is, David would pronounce, nothing truly to see in the clouds, only whatever we think we see, but isn't in fact really there to be seen. A fragment he once read somewhere surged into his mind: "The softness of the sky . . . the illusory meaning with which we had clothed it . . . " He had no desire to have the argument that he was sure would result, so instead he kept quiet and stared out the side window. He wondered what it was in others that made them so prone to take an innocent proposal about spotting shapes as an opportunity for criticizing belief in God. Although he himself had never seen a sign from heaven in the clouds, he would not scoff at somebody who said that he had.

Come to think of it, the atmosphere in the car reminded him of a similar ride once on a camping trip in the Sierra foothills with his friends and their fathers. As they were driving through intermittent thunder showers, his best friend's father, Robin, who had been driving, would look up to the sky, and with a silly face mockingly say, "Look, Son, it's raining! It's God!" Then the rain would stop, and the father would slip back into character, and say, "Look! The rain has stopped. It's God again!"

Even as a child without any religious indoctrination, he remembered being uncomfortable with the scene. There was something disturbing, even grotesque, about seeing a man angry like that at God. He remembered thinking to himself at the time how it was strange for his friend's father to mock God, when he claimed he didn't think God even existed. That was the first time he had seen someone who hated God, and as shocking as it was then, by now he was very used to it. He wondered whether his friends now here in the car had parents like Robin who had mocked God when they had been growing up. And he wondered what all of their childhood friends would say if they could see everyone in the car now. Would their own friends be surprised to see how they had turned out? He couldn't talk about any of this with them, as it would spoil the levity that everyone was hoping to procure from the afternoon. He tried cheering himself up, by reminding himself that he would soon be swimming. Thoughts about Calvin's doctrine of predestination and Schelling's notion of an eternal choosing of oneself outside time started to threaten to sprout further in his mind. When the ideas from various obscure textual passages he had once read began superimposing a pall of forebodingness over the pleasant country scenery, he sighed, and he swiftly banished them from further intruding.

He would concentrate on emptying himself of anything except what seeing the greenery would make him feel.

A crow was circling over the field. Watching it transported him to the Ile de la Cite on the Seine, where on Sunday afternoons people in Paris since the early nineteenth century would stroll through the island's exotic bird market. He imagined everyone in the car, Paul and Clara, Karl, Mick, and himself, strolling through the rows of cages, looking at the birds. He wondered which type of bird would be each of their favorites. He pictured Karl petting a blue parakeet, while two yellow canaries in the same cage sang their songs. Mick was enamored with a white bird that kept chirping its name: "Pierre, Pierre, Pierre." Out in the wild, the hawk now above the car would swoop down and eat the market's songbirds, but they were safe in their cages. He thought about the irony. People so often would talk about the great feeling of being freed like a bird flying from its cage. But maybe, sometimes, being trapped was a good thing, since at least it meant not being devoured by whatever might lurk outside. He thought about how one day it would be nice to walk in the market with whomever would be there to share the afternoon. He didn't know who she would be, or how he would meet her, but he felt sure that one day they would meet. He wondered what she was doing right now. If only it weren't for that Justice, he thought.

When they were nearly to the lake, Paul pulled the car off the highway, taking a wrong exit. As they reached the stop sign at the crest of the hill, there was a brown sign indicating the direction in which the Prison Museum was. As it happened, they were near where Texas performs its executions, and evidently there was a museum whose exhibits explored the stories of some of the state's most infamous murderers and their victims. Paul and Clara enjoyed being spontaneous, or at least cultivating the impression they were, so it made sense there would be an unexpected stop. This wasn't a wrong exit, after all, then.

Without any deliberation, his expectation of horizon shifted from what he would do when he got to lake, to what he would now be seeing at the museum in a minute or two. He had read voraciously about history when he was young, particularly military history, with all the stories of the Army Calvary on the Great Plains, or the Old Breed in the Pacific, or the Desert Fox in North Africa, or the Airborne at Bastogne. He thought about how Monty was overrated, something the disaster of Market Garden had finally proved, and how frustrating it was to see how Eisenhower and Bradley and the other generals had taunted Patton, when everyone had known how much they really needed him. For many years as an adolescent, he had thought he would join the military. That was before he came to decide that war was a scam, and that so much of politics is just a cartoonish story for the public to consume, and that only concealed what was really shaping the events over which he, and everyone else he knew, had no control. To be sure, he would never tell a veteran or a veteran's friends and family that the fighting had been for nothing, that all the men who had died had been duped, but he knew that if he ever had a son, he would be sure to warn him of the foolishness of war.

He thought of the time in seventh grade when a survivor from the Indianapolis, their history teacher's grandfather, had come to their class to speak to them about having been sunk at sea by a Japanese torpedo and then attacked by the sharks. Before he had come to tell the story, the man's granddaughter had mentioned that till this day her grandfather would never go in the ocean above the ankles. He thought about how all the men who had died horrible deaths out in the water were now forgotten, the only remaining trace of their former presence consisting in something like Quint's backstory in *Jaws*, events which, when the character relates them in the scene toward the end of the film, most people viewing today would probably think was something made up for the sake of the character's backstory, but which bore no relation to reality. It had all been a waste, he concluded, as they hopped out of the car, and entered the building.

In one display case was a shotgun and pistol that had been retrieved from the car in which Bonnie and Clyde were killed. That would have been roughly around the same time, only a decade beforehand, in fact, that her teacher's grandfather and his friends aboard the ship had found themselves floating in the Pacific. He wondered if all the men on the Indianapolis had known the story of Bonnie and Clyde, and how they had felt about it, if they did. Maybe, in fact, one of them had thought about the bank robbers, as he was floating in the ocean, doing what he could to distract himself from the fact that he might at any moment be pulled beneath the water and chomped to bits by one of the sharks brushing up against everyone's legs dangling under the surface of the water. He wondered what the probability associated with the possibility that one of the sailors did have such a thought. It was certainly greater than zero. And anything that wasn't an impossibility stood a chance of being actual. There was no way for anyone to know what the probability of one of the sailor's having had the thought was, but the fact that the precise likelihood of it eluded us, only in a way enhanced the feeling that it belonged to being, that it somehow counted for something, at least more than nothing at all. If the sailors were still alive today, he wondered what they would make of the fact that he was standing here in this museum looking at these guns, questioning whether everything he had heard from his teacher's grandfather about their experience out in the water during the war had been worth it. By now, most of the men from the Indianapolis, including the old man who had talked to them, were dead. Dead just like Bonnie and Clyde. Maybe everything under the sun really is vanity, he couldn't help but think, as he walked over to another exhibit.

Everyone from the car had fanned out and gone his own way once inside, but now they all happened to converge at a wall displaying a series of portraits with accompanying plaques. The photos, mostly in black and white, were of various Texas killers executed over the years. There was the obligatory biographical explanation of their life and crimes, and something of course about the time and method of their demise. But far more interesting, he thought, were the statements left by friends and family of the victims. While the plaques represented a range of views, the preponderance of them expressed feelings of capital punishment's inadequacies. Strikingly, above all, the families stated how seeing the murderer put to death didn't provide them the closure or sense of justice they had assumed that it would. They still felt empty. He had never been a strong advocate of capital punishment, though he conceded the role the desire for vengeance too often played in human affairs. In later years, when he had come to oppose capital punishment entirely, it wasn't because he denied its deterrent effects, or anything like that. If he had to explain himself to somebody, all he could simply say was that it just felt that keeping a man alive was a way of reminding everyone that in the end God will judge. It seemed to him that was the truly fearful thought. Maybe if society feared God more, there wouldn't be whatever need for executions those who supported them thought there is.

Without having to ask, he knew that his friends were also against the death penalty. He thought about mentioning he was too, since they would be surprised by that. But it all seemed otiose, so he didn't. Clara was drying the tears from her eyes, and Mick looked haunted by the familial testimonials, while Karl was leaning inches away from one portrait, as if he were counting the freckles on the murderer's face. He could understand opposing both the death penalty and abortion together, or else supporting them both, but he had never understood the contortions to which many people would go to support one but not the other. It was strange. Clara, like so many women her age, was perfectly capable of crying for an executed murderer, but she couldn't feel the slightest compassion for a baby murdered in an abortion. To her, one was clearly the victim of an inhumane and barbarous procedure, the other a total afterthought. He wondered why she could feel so differently about the two, and how she reconciled the inconsistency in her mind, or whether she had ever even tried.

"Well, uh, shall we?" Paul said, as he gestured blithely to the car, trying to dispel the heaviness that had settled over them all. The detour was now threatening to spoil the day's sense of adventure, so it was time to go.

FOUR

WHEN the car sped through the wooden gateway into the park, any lingering gloominess had nearly vanished, which was good, they all thought to themselves, because everyone was eager to forget what had been seen at the museum. They might talk about it later when they were all bored back in the city, but for now, for the rest of today, any debate about the ethics of killing or the meaning of death would have to wait.

Mick rolled the window down, leaned his head into the wind, and began barking like a dog. Clutching a bottle of Brut champagne resting on his lap, for a moment, it appeared he might open it while they were still driving. Paul followed suit, rolling his driver window down and yelping like an angry chihuahua. Karl sat motionlessly in silence, smiling in the middle seat. Karl wouldn't be barking, and neither would he. Up in the front passenger seat, Clara was staring into her side view mirror, looking to see what he would do. His window had already been rolled down for a while, so to make clear that his sympathies lay with Karl, and that he wouldn't be doing any barking either, he reached his arm fully out the window, flying his hand through the air like an airplane. He could tell she wanted to pressure him to bark also. She always did that thing girls do, trying to make him do something that she knew would make him uncomfortable, just to see whether he could be cajoled. But with Karl refusing as well, there would be no way to force him, so she didn't bother trying.

The other car was already there, with Cody, Tony, David, and Jack sitting in a circle around an empty fire pit, red plastic cups in hand. The pine trees provided some shade, the needles forming a prickly bed beneath their feet. The group was lounging in their shorts, with everyone but Tony shirtless.

"What took you guys so long?" Jack asked. "We thought you guys were lost."

Paul mumbled about stopping at the museum, but nobody wanted to know the details. It was the lake that mattered, and now they were mostly all here. Someone had put folk music on for ambience, the twang of the banjos and guitars mixing with the frog croaks and bird chirpings.

Hunching over, David lathered sunscreen on his wispy arms. He didn't look downward, but kept his gaze firmly ahead on Mick and Cody, both of whom were listening attentively to what David was saying, as they all drank their beers.

"No, no, he's completely different from Heidegger! He doesn't think the I-Thou relation is a structural feature of everything. He thinks it is a special type of encounter." David, obviously, was talking about Martin Buber, as was his habit. "It's not like Levinas, either," David clarified. For reasons he had never been quite able to understand, David loathed Levinas.

"C'mon, David, you're missing the point you know that I'm trying to make. Language is a system that determines thought. Buber's philosophy doesn't appreciate that. It's too Cartesian."

Mick, evidently, was deploying a rhetorical move from the latest poststructuralist text he had been reading over in the English department. Judging by the level of irritation in the Aussie's voice, and the fact that he had just used David's name, the two of them had both made their respective points a few times, yet neither was budging.

"Mick is right. Language is a system," Cody said flatly.

When, as now, he didn't feel like talking, he found it amusing to watch the various alliances emerge and shift through the course of one of the group's intellectual sparring sessions. In this case, despite the fact that Mick and Cody had entirely opposing views of the sense in which language was said to be a system, at this stage in the debate, they found themselves allies. He could see why. Hoping to parlay the observation about systematicity into a broader point about how everything, not merely language, was a Laplacian system of physical laws, Cody found it to his advantage to side with Mick. Jack, who was standing over at the bench fixing a hotdog, was listening intently, and, given the direction the discussion was now taking, he was almost certain to interject with a comment about Leibniz's doctrine of infinite analysis. It would be necessary, Jack would feel, to point out its relevance to the question at issue. He could see Jack nodding to himself, and, in his excitement to hurry to rejoin the conversation, he spilled some relish on his tank top. For his part, Karl, also a fellow Leibniz adept, detected the same argumentative opening as Jack. Rather than lunge in to interject as Karl might ordinarily, however, he quietly snorted at the conversation, turning to face the lake.

"Let's go swimming," Karl said almost to himself.

The others heard, and, judging by the shift in their postures, it was clear they realized a swim did make more sense than further soliloquies about language. But first, naturally, David was going to have to rest his case with a closing argument. Deftly anticipating the direction in which Cody had been hoping to steer the argument, David tactically conceded Mick's objection about the nature of language, but then countered by saying, "You're not seeing the point. Even if what you are claiming about language is true, Buber is talking about something more primordial. It isn't a linguistic encounter," he explained.

David, as usual, was seeking to occupy a middle intellectual space, one still preserving a space for genuine human meaning without endorsing the existence of a soul and God, yet at the same time resisting the idea that everything was as if nothing. As for Jack, his enthusiasm for the speculative metaphysics of early modern rationalism notwithstanding, he was sometimes inclined to claim that human experience was merely events in a central nervous system. So long as the grandeur of the logical and mathematical worlds were given their due credit, Jack didn't care so much about whatever else the others wanted to erase from their own ontological ledgers of reality. David, of course, knew all this. For Jack, Cody, Mick, and Tony, it had become second nature, during discussion at least, to discard themselves and everything they experienced for the sake of their preferred intellectual system.

Sensing he was surrounded on all sides, and that there was no way of pleasing anyone with his observation about Buber, David stood up, and as if it had been his own suggestion, said exasperatedly, "Oh, forget it. Let's go down for a swim."

Everyone walked to shore, left their towels on the white sand, and got in. The water was much warmer than they expected. Mick and Cody straightaway dove all the way in, and started kicking to reach the point where the bottom would give out beneath them, and they would be able to tread. Karl was already floating on his back closer to shore, while Jack,

David, and Tony were all standing waist deep together, skimming their hands along the surface of the water, occasionally splashing each other. Clara and Paul surfaced the farthest out, having swum out together as far as they could while holding their breath.

He stood in the water to his knees, pausing to take in the scene. Raising his hand above his brow for a visor, he stared up at the clouds above. Across the lake, on the opposite shore, perhaps a hundred yards away, was a cove whose lily pads caught his attention. It might be worth walking over to there later, assuming there was a road or trail.

To his immediate right, on the water's edge, stood a lifeguard tower. As a strong swimmer, he didn't see any danger posed by a placid lake, yet he supposed it was regulation that demanded there be one, anyway. It must have been the juxtaposition he noticed between the tranquility at the lake and the thought of the general possibility of drowning that led him in turn to think about how, for others at different times and places than this one, it had been in the water that they'd met death. Unexpectedly, his mind turned to the times when, as a child, his friend's father, Robin, would read stories to them before bed. One evening when they were eight, his friend's father read from the novel *Snow Falling on Cedars*. He remembered lying in the upper bunk riveted by Robin's solemn voice reading the harrowing account of Ishmael Chambers's experience of storming the beach as a young Marine at Tarawa. As he had understood at the time, his friend's father was trying to teach them raw lessons about life. The father knew, for instance, how they were young, and liked to play war, so he thought he would disabuse them of their fantasy that war was glorious, by showing that it was not beautiful at all. More importantly, the father knew how school had been teaching them that America was a land of freedom and justice, so he thought he would show them that the Japanese-Americans had been treated wrongly during the war. Is being forcibly relocated to an internment camp by one's own government freedom? Before reading the novel to them that night, Robin had at some point already told them the stories of how, when he himself had been a boy, he and his older brothers would explore the Oxnard dunes, where they would find old expended naval munitions buried in the sand. They didn't truly appreciate it at the time, the father had explained, that those shells had been designed to kill others. For what? We were told, as he said, that the bombs and bullets had been made to keep us all free, yet there wasn't any freedom for those who had been sent to the internment gaps, was there? As he would listen to his friend's father explain his vision of how the world really worked, he remembered watching the man's face twist into anger when he began recounting how his family had been rounded up by the government and sent away. Hearing the story as a young boy, he never doubted that the experience of injustice his friend's father related had been bad. Still, he felt like the bitterness he saw in the man wasn't truly because of Manzanar. Manzanar, it seemed to him, had given his friend's father the excuse he was looking for to be bitter. The anger the man had for the world was a way of avoiding addressing his anger with himself. He wondered if the father knew this about himself, knew what was really causing it.

Standing here in the water, he saw the element of wisdom in the man's flawed observations. It didn't make sense to say we had fought for freedom. That was true. Yes, about that, there could be no doubting he was correct. Setting aside the fact that not every American was free while the country was said to be fighting for freedom, there was the further question about what really would have happened, if those we had been told were our enemies had won. When he was a child, the answer he would hear at school had seemed straightforward. "Good thing we won the war, else we'd all be speaking Japanese or German right now," people would say on the Fourth of July, as the old phrase had it. But what of it? Germans didn't mind speaking German, just like Japanese didn't mind speaking Japanese. If we spoke something besides English, we'd speak it fine. He imagined for a moment the lifeguard's perch being a prison camp tower run by the Gestapo. If it were, what would that really change about the present moment? As long as they were still able to swim, it didn't matter what language the lifeguard spoke, or what language he and his friends spoke. Was freedom just being able to go swimming?

He thought about how swimming here today was, for him, an indulgence. Many lives on earth throughout history had elapsed from cradle to crave without leisure, though. For his teacher's grandfather from the Indianapolis, for instance, being at the lake today would be a terror. He stood still, waiting for a further thought to crystalize. The moment passed, nothing profound or perceptive having formed. All he knew is that he felt somehow unworthy of existence, guilty that for him life was so easy, that he could swim here in the lake without having to fear being carted off to Manzanar, or blown to bits by a mortal shell on the beach at Tarawa, or eaten by sharks out in the Pacific. There had been so much sacrifice, so much of it meaningless too, for him to be here in these circumstances, able to stand under the bright sun and clouds. He thanked God for being alive, for being here, and dove under.

FIVE

W HEN he surfaced from the water, it was near the diving platform. Mick and Jack did some somersaults, as Paul clapped
his hands, and the others looked on. After a few more rounds
of diving, Mick and Jack swam over to join the formation that everyone
had formed between the shore and the diving platform. They played games,
seeing who could hold his breath the longest, who could plunge all the way
to the bottom, or who could tread the longest with his arms held in the air.
There was splashing and laughing. By the time they finally came to shore to
gather their belongings, they were tired.

Tony walked to the fire pit and began changing into pants, while Paul
and Clara were busy fetching something from the car.

"Hey, did you guys see the other beach over there?"

He pointed to the distant cove. Jack and David nodded indifferently,
and turned to walk to the campsite to join Tony and Paul and Clara. Mick
and Cody, though, had apparently been eyeing the other shore also, because their attention piqued as soon as he mentioned it. But it was Karl
who looked the most intrigued. Everyone could tell when Karl had become
smitten with some idea, which, no matter how impractical or inconvenient,
he would see to accomplishing. Recognizing Karl's euphoria, Mick and
Cody seized on his mood, and began egging him on.

"Do it, Karl. Swim out there. It's pretty far. I bet you can't."

The four of them stood together on the beach, forming a line parallel
to the waterline, and stared out to the far shore. It was shaping up to be a
race, they realized.

Before there would be no turning back, Mick flinched. "You guys are
crazy," he laughed. "I'm going to get something to eat."

Cody waffled next, turning to follow Mick. Karl watched them walk away, then turned to him, "Well, guess it's just us."

Thinking Karl was still sincere about following through, he stepped into the water. He was about to dive.

"Wait! What are you doing? I was just kidding." He looked to see Karl shaking his head, as he sprinted to catch up with the others.

He realized that he had been frightened, though he hadn't noticed so until Karl had interrupted him. There was no reason to be scared, he told himself. The swim was some distance, but nothing unmanageable. He sighed deeply, told himself he may as well see what happens, and thus he began swimming, at first mainly using his legs to conserve his arm strength for later. As he passed beyond the platform, he flipped over to have a look toward shore. Everyone at the fire pit was staring. He waved to them all, but nobody waved. So far, at least, it was pretty easy going, so he saw no point in stopping. He kept swimming, using his arms as he lied on his back to kick with his legs. The water began changing slowly, first from its original translucent green to dark blue, and then again to a very dark blue. Soon he couldn't make out the shape of his own body beneath the surface. There was no telling how deep the water was below, and images of alligators and snakes began crossing his mind. He didn't think there were any alligators in the park, but he started to worry there could be, after it occurred to him that perhaps he had seen a warning sign about them when they had driven through the front gate. As he came closer to the cove's shore, his fear inten-sified, so strongly, in fact, that when he reached the lily pads that had once seemed so beautifully alluring from the beach, he couldn't wait to be done with them. Right as he was hoping that the hardest stretch of the swim was over, his arms began snagging against the weeds and plants. Some sort of thick grass was wrapping itself around his hands and arms, entangling him and making it hard to continue stroking. It was already too shallow to float and kick, yet too deep to stand easily. The water was splashing up his nos-trils. In a flash, he realized that he may be drowning, even though he was so close to shore. The day's thoughts about sharks were not helping, either. He felt he would be in the teeth of an alligator any second, dragging him down into the weeds, never to be seen again. He pulled himself through the last of the lily pad death trap, and washed onto the sand.

He didn't know how long he had been swimming aside from the fact that it had taken longer than he'd anticipated it would. And he understood that the others had been reasonable not to attempt the swim. Above all, he knew they would be angry that he had, and because he didn't want to anger them any more than he knew they'd already be, when he stood up to walk off the beach, he made sure not to look out across the lake to them, lest it be perceived as gloating. He knew they had seen him make it.

He cut through some light shrubbery into the pines, struggling to catch his breath. There was a dirt road heading in the direction of the main entrance. He figured he could follow it for as long as it let him hug the shore and keep the destination in sight. Judging by the sun, it was probably around four, so he didn't have to be in any rush to get to the camp. They'd be at the park a while before having to leave. He took a breath to calm down.

Typically, it wouldn't have been an issue, since he would have taken care of it while still in the lake, but in the initial effort to swim out, and then the frenzy that arose close to shore, he found it necessary to step behind a tree and attend to business. As he was urinating, he tried to avoid hitting any of the ants he saw marching along the tree on route to their fortress kingdom somewhere in the brush. He was not a Jansenist by any stretch, but he always had instinctively disliked killing bugs senselessly. He never had understood the mentality of others whose natural response to seeing a bee, or a spider, or whatever, was to kill it. Thinking about it, people crush bugs without remorse mainly just because they are small. But that didn't make any sense. Why was it okay to crush another creature simply because it happened to be small? He surmised that people's reasoning was that, because a bug was small, it probably didn't have a consciousness, or at least not any sentience of substantial significance. But that was an obvious leap in logic. He didn't mean to criticize those who kill bugs thoughtlessly, but he did think that, here again, they were being dishonest with themselves. After all, if a race of massive giants came to earth, it wouldn't be any defense on their part to claim they were justified in squashing humans because humans were tiny to them. A human being's life would remain exactly what it is now, no matter how big a giant came along to observe it.

The more he considered it, he was sure his views about bugs implied he shouldn't eat meat, and while he didn't begrudge vegetarians himself, he did find the outspoken among them irritating. He found them annoying, not so much because he thought they were mistaken to say eating meat was bad, but because, if one looked, one was sure to discover any number of inconsistencies and hypocrisies in their own lives and beliefs. There were probably many vegetarians, for instance, who didn't have the slightest qualms about squashing a bug when one happened to crawl up their arm, or tried to land on their head.

In the final analysis, he supposed, it was possible to view all of existence as God's creation, a natural cathedral, which probably rendered the majority of what everyone ordinarily does wrong, he concluded. When he had been younger, he had entertained the idea of entering a monastery. His father encouraged it, because he thought it was impossible for a man to go wrong when he honestly followed his heart, but his mother kept that thick silence she would whenever she meant to discourage somebody whom she thought was doing or saying something crazy. As he sauntered along the road winding through the trees, he accepted that he was not a monk, and that almost certainly he would never be, but he didn't think it was so strange to consider the possibility that everyone could be less cavalier in the way they kill bugs.

By now, the walk was taking longer than he had anticipated it would. Apparently, the swim had traversed a far greater distance than he had judged. When he at last reached the campsite, he had been gone for long enough that it felt a bit like stepping into a home village that had forgotten its itinerant son, having taken the old traveler long ago for dead or missing. Nobody looked up to say a word. He grabbed a chair from the picnic bench, set it down in the ring with the others, and tried to orient himself in relation to where the conversation had led without him. After what had been one of their collective exchanges replete with its typical twists and turns, asides and digressions, clarifications and qualifications, questions and assertions, wisecracks and insults, there was no way of knowing the precise details of what had been said. At any rate, perhaps it didn't matter, since by then, nothing seemed to have changed. They were back to Buber.

"I know, I know, I'm a broken record," David said to everyone with a smug look on his face.

David knew everyone knew Buber was his idol, a topic to which he could endlessly return whenever he felt socially uncomfortable. But of course, as David well knew they knew, they all did the very same thing, Jack and Karl with Leibniz, Mick with Derrida, Cody with Nelson Goodman. Everyone had to indulge the others, if he was to expect the others to indulge him.

"Now again, as I was saying, the point is that the I-Thou relation . . . "

His attention shifted from David and the others sitting in the ring around the pit. He smiled to himself while looking out onto the water. Maybe he would see her again tonight.

Six

"OKAY, cool. See you all there," he said, as he turned to the street, leaving the backyard behind him.

After having pulled up to the garage at Paul and Clara's place, they had unpacked the coolers and chairs, thrown out the trash from the outing, and made plans for the night. After a brief set of deliberations, it had been decided that they could all first go home, shower and change, and then meet up again by ten or eleven. Paul suggested Rudyard's, but nobody was in the mood for something quiet and out of the way, so they'd decided on the bar he'd been at Tuesday. The schedule would be tight, but probably there would be one of the large tables available for them, hopefully one outside in the back. Due to the bar opening the space outside, which had formerly been a large residential backyard and had been renovated, the capacity had increased, and the crowds had been growing over the past few weekends. Word was out, among all the students and young locals, that this was the spot to be. There were frequently now long lines at the front door, and standing room only inside and outside. No doubt the bar would be jammed tonight.

"If you get there before me, get two rounds of Tecate and whiskey!" Jack hollered out.

Jack didn't like crowds. Ordinarily, Jack would never be going out on a Saturday night, but it being the special occasion it was owing to Mick's birthday and with everyone else going, even Karl would be there, he was making an exception. If Jack didn't want to be left drinking at his house alone, it would be necessary to tag along with the group. And if Jack couldn't help that it would be busy, he would have to plan accordingly.

"Will do," he said, turning his head to Jack in the yard.

Leaving the house, he was acutely aware that there was less banter than before when in the afternoon they had been preparing to head for the lake. It wasn't simply that everyone was tired, he knew. There was a lingering tension from the lake, as evidently his swim across the lake had ruffled feathers, particularly with Cody, but because everyone couldn't deny that the entire thing really was nothing to be upset about, by the time they all got to the bar, everything would be in fine shape again, it seemed to him. To try to help soothe things, he had decided that walking home was better than asking anyone for a lift, since doing so might avoid the appearance of being rude for expecting a ride. It was only a mile or two, the route taking him through the city's charming Museum District, which he liked. He always enjoyed the sight of the homes surrounding his apartment, with their royal oaks and rolling lawns.

Seeing his gesture's rationale, Clara had nodded to him approvingly, as if to so say thank you, but she didn't say so aloud for fear of infuriating Cody, whom she knew would see it as a betrayal. He wondered whether Paul was aware yet that Cody had his eyes on Clara. Before he could think more about it, however, Tony called to him, as they were walking to the street.

"Sure that you don't need a ride, dude?"

"Oh, no, don't worry about it. I'll be fine. Thanks, though."

He meant what he said, as did Tony. And yet, there was still that inevitable awkwardness everyone feels when someone is being relieved of the opportunity to do a nicety. When he reached the empty lot on the corner overgrown with weeds, Tony's car stopped at the intersection. The left turn signal began flashing. "See you later," Tony waved out the window.

The car made the left, while he went right, walking along the sidewalk. It was after dinnertime, so when he reached the main street, the restaurants were largely empty. It was still early enough in the evening for the bars to be empty also. Things were quiet, and he liked it.

Two blocks from the apartment, he passed the big, empty lot whose home was recently demolished. He thought about what it would be like, to be wealthy enough to purchase a mansion, knock it down, and then build a new one. He wasn't envious of that life. Just curious. In fact, merely imagining what it would be like for such a life to be his own made him shudder. As undeniably beautiful as many of the houses in the neighborhood were, they had a certain despair about them, as if they were more so mausoleums than they were homes. Tombs for the living dead, monuments to frustrated desire, he thought to himself. Looking at the empty lot, he recalled that Carrell, his advisor, had mentioned how he and his wife, Laura, had recently purchased a new property in the neighborhood. They were excited to be designing their dream home from scratch, Carrell had said. This must be the place, then. He leaned against the chain-link fence, putting his hands through the holes, and stared at the pit of dirt where the workmen would soon be pouring the foundation. The famous Bible verse occurred to him, "A foolish man, who built his house on sand . . . "

His own apartment complex, which was neither exclusive nor expensive, was a relic from the fifties, a historic property that in all likelihood would soon be demolished by developers looking to attract the young professionals from the Northeast who were beginning to relocate to the city for their companies who had been opening offices here. For now, though, the building stood. When he arrived, he nodded to three neighbors who were drinking iced tea in the courtyard.

"Beautiful," he said pointing to the sea of white clovers that had sprouted in the yard from the rain.

"Yes, it's easy to forget they're weeds," one of the women said laughingly. He went inside.

"Dude, come in here. I have to show you something."

It was Timothy waving an arm, standing outside his unit down the hall. He had a huge knowing smile on his face, like the Cheshire cat, suggesting a supreme confidence that what he was about to show would be worth seeing. He checked his phone for the time, and seeing it was now nine-thirty already, decided that there would be no time to shower. He would throw on a collared shirt before he and Timothy left for the bar—judging by his friend's demeanor, it appeared safe to assume he would want to come.

"One second," he said.

He stepped into his apartment, put on a light blue button-down, grabbed a sixpack from the kitchen counter, locked his door behind him, and walked down the hall to where Timothy stood waiting.

Timothy slapped his shoulder as they walked in. Since the last time he had been inside, the furniture had been rearranged completely. Evidently, Timothy had meant to consolidate everything, including his bed, in the living room. It would be too hard to weave through the clutter, so instead he plopped himself down on a bean bag chair in the corner. Timothy took a seat on the bed and grabbed the remote. He clicked a button, and a video on the wide screen on the wall began playing. A fit elderly Italian man dressed in traditional Japanese Samurai attire swung a large blade inside a bowling alley, performing a series of impressive technical moves with his sword to the accompaniment of a dramatic drumming soundtrack.

"Isn't that so awesome?" Timothy asked when it was over.

It was an interesting performance, but nothing nearly worthy of the absolute awe with which Timothy was treating it. His friend must have been smoking marijuana, he saw.

"Yeah, that's cool. Want a beer?" he said, trying delicately to change the subject.

Timothy leapt from the bed, grabbed two, cracked one open, chugged it down, dropped the can on the floor, and then, without looking, fell backwards onto the bed, as if he were cave jumping. "Woooooo," he exclaimed.

He thought about extricating himself, in order to leave for the bar alone. But then he felt guilty at the idea, and, deciding it might be good for Timothy to get out of the apartment, he mentioned everyone's plans to meet at the bar.

"Want to go?" he asked.

"Oh, yeah, definitely, man. Lemme get ready."

Timothy was already dressed, so it wasn't clear what exactly he intended to do. He stood up and walked over to a desk at the window. Fumbling through the drawers, he pulled out a chess board.

"It's going to be super busy tonight. I don't think there'll be room for the board," he said diplomatically to Timothy.

He could see Timothy momentarily escape his false euphoria, as a look of clarity came over his face. Although there was some embarrassment in his eyes, his friend seemed relieved to be calm.

Timothy looked gently at him, "Yes, thanks. Good point. We can play later tonight when we're back."

He himself wasn't a good chess player. Their matches were always preordained Timothy victories, but at least playing gave them something good to do together, and it helped Timothy put his mind on something concrete, where for a time he could collect himself, and reconnect to the world. He in college had once seen another friend descend into schizophrenia, and he worried that potentially was happening here. Although society would classify Timothy's behavior as mad, and it certainly was, there was something profound to him about the fact that a burgeoning madman was the one who could see, clearer than anyone, the irrationality of what those around them accepted as normal, but wasn't normal at all. A remark he'd read somewhere about madness came to mind: "The veils of universal occlusion seem to part and penetrating truths are manifested . . . The beginning of certain mental disorders are marked by shattering metaphysical revelations . . . " That was Jaspers, he thought. In any case, the two insanities were different, of course, each capable of unmasking the other for what it was. He wondered what reality truly was, if neither Timothy's perception nor the everyday world which Timothy rightly saw to be phony, were reality. Was everything an illusion? Even though the conclusion seemed to force itself on him presently, he resisted it, recalling his earlier thoughts about it from Tuesday which he believed then had shown otherwise. Perhaps reality was refusing to get drawn into either illusion, to resist the delusion that the everyday was rational, on the one hand, but to also resist the dissolution that came with rejecting it in the fashion Timothy was, on the other. As to where exactly recognizing the world was a lie was supposed to leave him, he was unsure. The line about existing from Kierkegaard sprang to his mind, "to remain out over the deep, over seventy thousand fathoms . . . "

"Ready. Let's go," Timothy said.

He walked through the door, Timothy's footsteps plodding behind him. When they reached the building door, he glanced over his shoulder, and saw Timothy's door had been left ajar. He pointed.

Timothy laughed. "Oh, yeah, whatever, don't worry about it. It'll be fine."

His friend put on a goofy face, and began pretending to prowl around the hallway like a burglar, the impersonation suggesting that anyone sincerely interested in breaking into the apartment and stealing something was only an imbecile worthy of mocking. For a moment, he seriously worried that Timothy, in order to prove his indifference's sincerity, might start stacking up all his belongings outside the doorway in the hallway. As they walked outside, Timothy plopped the remaining beers from the sixpack on the table where the neighbors were sitting. It could have been a nice gesture, but in this case, it misfired badly, since Timothy, already preoccupied with whatever was flying through his mind, failed to notice that the others were drinking iced tea, not alcohol, for a reason. Too embarrassed to say no thank you, they all smiled uncomfortably, and told Timothy and him to have fun. For a second, he thought about telling Timothy he had changed his mind, and turning around and just going to bed. He wasn't sleepy, but he suddenly was tired and felt like being alone.

Seven

T HE walk to the bar was short, and it felt so, with Timothy talking the entire time to distract him. Or, nearly distracting him. The sudden fatigue which had overtaken him at the apartment was fading, but not yet fully. He felt an immense indifference to the night that lay ahead, to everything, frankly. He wondered why, if he in one sense had no desire to be doing what he was doing, he did it. Then again, maybe he was doing what he desired to do. After all, he was doing it. Was it even coherent to posit the notion of doing something he didn't desire to do? If he didn't desire to do it, then why did he do it?

As he felt the mood of ennui finally begin to scatter to the winds, he wondered whether there was truly a metaphysical mystery here, or whether he was simply being taken in by some sort of semantic confusion at work in the use of the word "desire." There were those, of course, some of his friends among them, who would assert the problem was entirely dissolvable in another way, since according to them, there was in principle no difference between doing something one desired, and doing something contrary to what one desired, since what anyone did do, in either case, wasn't up to anyone anyway, the experience of free choice being nothing more than an illusion. "When I deliberate the die is already cast . . . " Was that Murdoch, he wondered? He quickly admonished himself for that bad habit of always seeking to label a thought of his with the name of someone else. The train of reflection proceeded. Go to the bar, and he will regret it; do not go to the bar, and he will regret it—either way, he will regret it, and either way, he is mistaken for doing so, since as there is no real choice, it is foolish to regret doing anything at all. Hence, when one fully thought it through, it follows that the illusion of agency was itself a license to exercise it, not however one pleased, since technically on this view nobody did exercise agency anyway, but, well, setting that little difficulty aside, the point was simply not to worry about anything, much less regret it, since it didn't really matter. His mind turned to a class he'd taken once on Kant, Hegel, and Nietzsche as an undergraduate. Phil Horowitz, the instructor, who had spent his early scholarly years at Dartmouth, told them all a funny story meant to illustrate the aporia. He recalled Horowitz recounting to them the story of how one time, on the last day of the quarter, a student streaked naked through the room exclaiming, "I'm free! I'm free! See, I'm free!" When the student ran out, Horowitz had said that he turned to the class and remarked, "That doesn't prove anything other than he was determined to do it." When Horowitz told them the story, everyone had erupted in laughter. Now in retrospect, he realized his teacher had probably made up the whole story, but at least the apocryphal streaker had been used to illuminate an interesting point about the problem of free will.

The perennial problem of free will, a mystery. Whether it was even a legitimate problem was itself a matter of dispute, as he knew from the vast reading he had done on the subject. His mind turned to Schelling. Or rather, he recalled what Heidegger had written somewhere about Schelling: "The feeling of the fact of freedom means the direct experience that we are free. But Schelling also makes us consider that this fact does not lie on the surface to that extent so that we could find the appropriate words for it instantly, words which could tell us what this being free really is." Maybe that was right. Perhaps we didn't fully comprehend the concept of freedom itself. Another passage from the same text floated to consciousness. If we inquired sufficiently deeply into the concept of human freedom, he recalled it saying, "the illusory question about freedom of the will which continually plays havoc in doctrines of morality and law would have long since disappeared, and it would become evident that the real question about freedom is something quite different from what is talked about in the 'problem of freedom of the will.'" That, however, seemed wrong to him. There could well be more to freedom than the traditional philosophical formulation of the problem suggested, but the problem of the will itself was not entirely illusory, he thought.

He considered asking Timothy whether he thought they were free, but he decided not to ask. Maybe he would bring it up later, when they were all at the bar, and there was a lull in the conversation. David would probably make the ensuing discussion a miserable one, but it might be worth bringing up nonetheless.

Rather than pass through the park with the fountain, they came up the street from another direction. Just as they had expected, there was a giant line forming, stretching down to the car repair shop on the next lot. The doorman was ordering the line to form in that direction rather than the other, in order to try to minimize noise from reaching the house immediately next door, which was a residential home. Its occupants' patience must understandably be wearing thin. The bar had been receiving noise complaints on the weekends for good reason. Rumors were circulating that the fire marshal was going to be dispatched at some point soon, as the crowds exceeded what the city occupancy laws permitted. The resulting scene before them, which looked exactly like what happens when a crowd the size of the concert is crammed into a modest two-story house, was a bubble about to burst, and everyone could feel it, which only added to the urgent atmosphere of everyone there trying to savor nights like these while they still lasted. Most likely, this would be the last weekend before the authorities would shut it down.

The bass thumping from the stereo out back made it almost impossible to hear anything out front. Timothy, who was walking by those already waiting in line, headed off to grab a spot at the end of the line, which extended all the way to the street corner.

"Hey, wait a second, Timothy," he said. He couldn't tell whether his words were heard.

Looking up to the door from the foot of the stairs, he recognized the doorman checking IDs. It wasn't the same doorman from Tuesday, but another one, Rusty, an affable roughneck who worked on the oil rigs in the Gulf, while working here at the bar part-time. They weren't close enough to be considered friends, but they had a rapport. He could tell Rusty saw working at the bar as only temporary, and although Rusty himself never said so, he saw that Rusty respected that he appeared to have no intention of becoming a lifer here, either. Rusty himself was perhaps oblivious to it, but the fact that Rusty always wore a plain white shirt was not just a matter of style, he thought. Or, more exactly, to the extent that it was so, it was a sign, whether Rusty realized it or not, that he wanted to be pure, that he believed the light was stronger than the darkness. He had met plenty of people, particularly in academia, who regularly wore black shirts for what seemed to him to be the opposite sentiment. Rusty ushered in a group of revelers, and turned to see whose turn was next.

"Hey man, what's up," Rusty said.

"Hey. About to grab a spot in line," he said.

Rusty smiled, and nodded toward the open door. Timothy, who was looping back to the front of the line, curious as to what was going on, saw they were being waved through. "Oh, awesome. Let's go!"

His friend sprinted up the stairs, threw his arms up in triumph when he reached the landing, striking the pose of an Olympic champion. Rusty chuckled, and shook their hands. The two walked in together, happy to have avoided the wait.

Some girls who had followed in behind them tried getting Timothy's attention, assuming Timothy had been waved in meant he might also be able to get them free drinks. Timothy stopped to chat with them at the door, which itself was near the staircase leading upstairs. He began stammering, losing his train of thought, as he was jostled by the flood of people careening up and down the stairs. He tapped Timothy on the shoulder, nodded hello to the girls, and led his friend gently to the counter.

"Four Tecates and whiskey, please," he told Billy.

"Sorry, we don't have Tecate."

"Oh, that's right. Lone Star then."

Timothy raised his eyebrows. "Double-fisting it tonight?"

"No, one round for you, one for me, and two for Jack. He asked me to order for him when we got here."

When he finished his sentence, he realized Jack and Timothy may not yet have met. He was about to ask Timothy whether they had, when he could see that Timothy wasn't interested in saying more about it anyway, so they grabbed their beers and whiskey, pressed them against their chests, and squeezed through the crowd to the side exit leading to the back patio.

They were just in time. Only one table was left open. They took a seat across from one another, elbows against the fence, their other drinks placed next to their sides to signal the spots beside them were taken. If anyone asked whether the rest of the table were open, they would say no. It would keep the crowd at bay for a while, but if the others didn't show up soon, they would have to hand the seats over.

He felt his phone vibrate. It was Rebecca.

"Plans tonight?"

Maybe she wanted to see him, or maybe she just wanted to test whether he did, but in any event, it was immaterial, since he had no intention of changing his mind about not pursuing things. It seemed like only trouble.

"Who's that?" Timothy asked.

"Some girl. Not going to answer. She'll probably end up here tonight, anyway."

Odds were that if one of Rebecca's friends saw them here, as her friend had on Tuesday, they would report back to her, and some kind of encounter would inevitably follow. He wondered whether Timothy might like her, in which case he could introduce them, but he reminded himself that Timothy wasn't in any condition to be meeting someone when he was barely hanging on at medical school. He scanned the crowd and wondered how many others there tonight were in bad shape too, fundamentally in no condition to be here, but still there anyway. He felt like he wasn't among them. Still, he had to admit they probably thought the same about themselves. How was anyone to know?

Although he didn't think it was an excuse for anyone's behavior, he did think much of the dysfunction in everyone's lives could very plausibly be traced to childhood trauma. It only made sense, he thought. That an experience was no longer figuring as an occurrent thought in consciousness, or as a recurrent one, or even as a potential one, didn't seem to him to forbid it from structuring somebody's encounter with the world. He had not read any Freud or Lacan extensively, but from what he had gleaned from others, it sounded like there was something to the psychoanalytic hypothesis. An experience from childhood was retained in memory, not in the way a document lying in a filing cabinet waiting to be retrieved is retained, but in the more primordial sense entailing that, once it had entered someone's consciousness, it left its mark, like a stamp that bears a seal. Receding into apparent oblivion, the experience would always still be there, if only by operating in the recesses of the mind, as it were. He himself had never been to see an analyst, and he had no desire to do so. He would not say it to others, because he knew it would be unkind, but he had a visceral suspicion of those who did go to therapy. He conceded to himself the potential inconsistency on his part. After all, if he was sympathetic to the psychoanalytic suggestion, according to which the unconscious structures much of one's interpretation of the world, then in principle he shouldn't be hostile to the idea that psychotherapy could help somebody manage whatever that meant in their lives. He couldn't articulate it persuasively, yet if had to try, his basic feeling was that there must be a better way to deal with whatever therapy attempted to address.

When he was younger, his mother would complain about her sisters, telling him that only losers and quitters went to therapists. Maybe that was why he had developed the antipathy to it he had. But although his mother's opinion may have been too sweeping of a generalization, her assessment accurately captured what he had observed anecdotally.

His thought turned to a time when he was ten or so. It was a summer afternoon at his best friend's house. His friend's mother entered the room to interrupt their playing, telling him that he would have to go home, because his friend had a therapy appointment. He remembered being unsettled. He had not known his friend was seeing a therapist, and he didn't really understand what a therapist even was, but he felt sure that his friend's mother seemed to have a strange need to mention it. He went home worrying about what possibly could be wrong with his friend. The most disconcerting thing of all, really, was that his friend seemed perfectly fine to him. He remembered feeling that his friend being sent to therapy had more to do with his friend's mother's own problem, than it ever had anything to do with his best friend. Thinking about it here years later, that still seemed correct.

Sitting at the crowded bar, he could see the childhood insecurities and pains etched on the faces of those around him. Time didn't obliterate it. It was all there, just in ways that weren't obvious. His same childhood best friend, for instance, had moved to New York City a few years ago to finish college. His friend had told everyone he was there to study marketing, yet secretly his friend confided to him what anyone could see was the case anyway, that he was there to break into the entertainment industry. It wasn't a preposterous notion, as if his friend were proposing jumping to the moon. From the time they were boys, everyone had seen his friend was a very gifted artist. His father, Robin, the one who read to them about Tarawa, was himself a sculptor and the owner of an art studio. By any reasonable measure, his friend's father was a success. But his friend's mother was never satisfied with her husband, and he remembered how frequently she would comment critically about the family's finances, suggesting to anyone that would listen how what her husband did was impractical, maybe even selfish. From the time they were young, she had attempted to steer her son away from art, pressuring him to do something else. Marketing, then, was simply his friend's way of appeasing his mother, as his friend sought out what he really wanted to do.

His friend wouldn't tell anybody that he wanted to be an actor or maybe a model. But despite being as extremely handsome as he was, with dreamy brown eyes and a square jaw, he was too short. The first time he visited his friend in New York, his friend had told him how everyone at the parties had been saying he could be a model, if only he weren't short. They had meant to compliment him. It was understandable, however, that it hurt him to hear it. After that first year, there was a stint where he had tried writing a screenplay. Around that same time, he landed a job working as a production assistant on a Scorsese film. He had seen his friend's pictures from the set of the crew having a squirt gun fight with Leonard DiCaprio. Then suddenly the film dream faded, without his friend ever giving any explanation. Ever since, it had been a string of office jobs. Perhaps his mother had threatened to cut him off financially.

Those in New York who did not know his friend's childhood experience and family life could in a way never really understand him. They would not know about their new friend's ambivalence to art, owing to his father's journey as an artist, nor would they know about his mother's attempts to guilt him into taking a different path. To those who thought they knew his old friend, he went by the nickname "Moto," and that was who they thought he was. They had no idea of how many times he had tried reinventing himself, or of how all those failed previous attempts at self-transformation had stemmed from a hidden conflict within himself, one which he would never tell anyone. The exception, he thought, was a therapist. His old friend would tell a therapist. Perhaps therapy, then, he concluded, was the one setting where people felt able to discuss who they really were, or really wanted to be, since everything else about their adult lives was little more than playing a role. We traumatized children in big bodies, he concluded.

EIGHT

"ARE these seats taken?"

There was frustration in the man's voice. It was only eleven forty-five, and while the bar usually was the kind of place that never was full until after midnight, owing to its swelling popularity in recent weeks, tonight it was already over capacity. There was hardly any room to stand, so everyone was eyeing the table. It wouldn't be long before a group tired of watching the space go to waste commandeered it. As Timothy and he were about resigned to giving up, Paul came barging out the side door, ambling down the rampway, a handful of beers in hand. Clara and Jack emerged next, and then, a second later, Mick too. The four of them pushed through the phalanx of bodies hovering over the table, and sat down, Mick and Jack next to him, Paul and Clara next to Timothy. No one had met his neighbor, and it took them all a moment in the drunken commotion to realize Timothy was sitting with them. He was about to introduce them, when Timothy introduced himself, sticking out his hand to each of them in turn.

"Hi, I'm Timothy. Good to meet you," he said bashfully. It appeared the mania was subsiding. He was almost serene.

Timothy's gesture of politeness went unnoticed. Jack and Mick, both of whom had been drinking before arriving, were bellowing. "For he's a jolly good fellow, for he's a jolly good fellow, for he's . . . " they sang, as Paul joined in, "a jolly good felloooow, which nooooobody can deny!"

Amused with themselves, they high fived each other, Jack wheezing from the smoking and laughing. When there was an interlude in the shenanigans, he offered Jack the two rounds of Lone Star and whiskey. It took Jack a moment to recall his earlier request.

"Oooh, awesome, thanks man." Jack took a sip of the beer. "Ugh," he said wincing, "it's lukewarm." He didn't remind Jack that they were late. Jack didn't seem to notice it was Lone Star rather than Tecate.

When they were this inebriated, Paul would adopt the identity of a character he had invented, an alternate personality, who spoke with a quiet raspy voice and mumbled perverted ramblings. It was a performance that embarrassed Clara more than it probably should. She called the persona "Uncle Paulie," and if the past were any reliable indication, by the looks of it, Uncle Paulie would be making an appearance very shortly. There wasn't anything particularly grating about Paul's recurring joke, he thought, and although it was undoubtedly immature, that wasn't especially off-putting either. If he thought about it, the bothersome thing was the sadness in it. Having to watch Paul slip into Uncle Paulie was like being forced to watch a depressed clown making dark jokes about himself. The self-loathing was too much.

He didn't notice David until he was standing at the end of the table. David looked at the seating arrangement, rubbing his chin ironically, as if in deep thought, and then plopped down next to Paul, patting him on the back. "I heard from Cody. He and Tony aren't coming. Neither is Karl," David said.

The table was stunned, especially Mick. Rather than explain why the others had said they weren't coming, David leaned forward to see Clara fully.

With a mordant smile, he said, "Looks like Uncle Paulie is gonna come out tonight, eh, Clara?"

Clara rolled her eyes, and the table laughed nervously, including Paul, who, sensing David's sarcasm, tried to lighten the mood by immediately launching into the character.

As the embarrassment unfolded, he turned away from Paul, and diverted his attention to the large apartment building down the street. Some of the lights were on, especially in the large penthouse suites on the upper floors. He himself had never been inside the Millrose Tower. But he had walked past it countless times. It was an open secret that the luxury apartment building was a notorious hub for energy executives and other wealthy businessmen to keep their mistresses, or to steal away to see prostitutes. Calling to mind his old friend's comments about corporate espionage and blackmail, he realized that many of the sleazy executives who were cheating on their wives there tonight must have no idea they were being filmed surreptitiously, and would not know so, until it was already too late. Then they were forever leverageable, ever susceptible to looking the other way from corruption, since not playing along to get along would consequently lead to an embarrassing disclosure that would mean both personal and professional destruction. Of course, for extortion and blackmail to work, law enforcement would have to be corrupt too, since if it weren't, anyone could simply go to the police, but since blackmail was obviously an effective means of control, evidently the police were indeed rotten, too. That would explain why places like this one could get away with turning a blind eye to the drug-dealing. When everyone is dirty, nobody wanted to report anything to anyone, because there was always the risk that in doing so one might only destroy oneself in the process. He sighed when contemplating the scale of the world's corruption. He felt glad that he could more or less keep to himself, and not have to worry about it. Even though nobody talked about it openly, he wondered if others knew about it too, but like him were simply happy to pretend it didn't exist.

He was bored, so he figured he would test it. "Hey guys, what do you think about blackmail?" he asked the table.

"What do you mean?" Mick asked. He laid out what he had in mind.

"That's stuff from the movies. I mean, I'm sure it happens, but it's not common," Jack said.

"How do you know?" he asked Jack, without any edge to his voice.

"Don't be paranoid. Of course, it's not common," Jack replied.

"You didn't answer my question. I asked how you know it's as rare as you think."

David started cackling. "Oh, boy, here we go. Always with the crazy stuff."

"And always the denial, with you," he fired back.

He felt himself getting angry, which he knew was what David wanted, since that would be the most effective way for David to divert everyone from the topic. He didn't think David was naïve enough to believe the world didn't contain the sort of sinister forces Jack was denying that it did. He didn't think David himself was likely to have any personal connections to such activity. There must be some psychological motivation for David's playing dumb. It could be something as simple as the fact that, having successfully tweaked Mick, Clara, and Paul since arriving, he was now next on David's list. But there seemed to be more to David's resistance.

He decided to test a hypothesis. "You just deny all this kind of stuff, because it would force you to admit the existence of evil," he said.

David slapped his knee and laughed dismissively. "Why would I want to deny that? I'm the last person who would. Religion scholars deal with the question of evil seriously all the time."

He had been intending to work his way to the point more slowly, so that when he finally made it explicit, everyone would see that David had no way to wriggle out of it, but since David had already unwittingly made his point for him, he figured he'd highlight it now.

"So, really, you don't dispute that you deny the existence of evil. When you say evil's a question, what you mean is that it's a phenomenon you treat as a scholarly topic of examination, which is just to say you treat it from within a theoretical framework that makes no genuine room for the supernatural existence of evil. And in any case, the upshot is that it's something you ignore practically."

He used the word "supernatural" for a reason, knowing it would negate the immediate response David would likely have wanted to make.

"Religious studies, like anthropology and other disciplines, approaches things without any commitment to the reality of what it studies. It tries to be neutral."

"Right. That's my point. You think you can study evil from a naturalistic framework."

"Not necessarily naturalistic."

"Okay, fine. A framework in which the supernatural, as traditionally understood, is rejected."

"We don't reject the supernatural per se. What you mean by traditional is probably loaded with a number of assumptions that scholars would challenge, so from a certain perspective, there's nothing orthodox, or deserving of default acceptance, of what you mean by the supernatural."

"Do you believe there's a devil?"

"It depends what you mean."

"I can tell you what I mean. But first tell me if you believe in a devil, however you understand him."

"Well, to begin with, I would not refer to the devil as a 'him.' I mean, it's probably already too much of an assumption to refer to the devil as an entity at all, much less a person, much less a male person."

"So you don't believe there's a devil."

"No, it's not that simple. Maybe, I do, like Ivan did."

"Sure, it is. You just provided me a definition of the devil you say you reject as being inadequate to understanding whatever else it is to which you think the concept might properly refer. But the bottom line is that you deny the devil exists. At least as I understand it."

"Just because I reject a monotheistic, or really Christian, concept of the devil is fine. The devil doesn't name an entity. It's just another way of naming . . . "

"Evil?" he asked. "So, then, I take it that at least you do believe evil exists. In which case it's simply a question of its scale." By now, the table was quiet.

"No, that's not what I said. Here again, it's more complicated than you're making it out to be. I probably reject a certain idea of evil you have, but that doesn't mean I believe there is no evil," David said.

"So if you admit there's evil, however you want to define it, then why is everyone acting like Jack has a point when he states it's somehow inconceivable that things like blackmail, extortion, and systemic corruption exist? If evil is part of the world, then it's hardly crazy that it would be widespread. So what's so hard about thinking that kind of stuff is common? Jack said I'm paranoid for thinking it's common, and I said he didn't know that. As far as I can tell, after all this arguing, nobody's any closer now to proving it is uncommon than they were ten minutes ago."

Timothy had been sitting silently the entire time. "Obviously there's evil. There probably even is a devil. What's the point in arguing? I mean, look around," he said laughing.

His comment was meant to highlight the stupidity of society, not necessarily its wickedness, but the effect was the same, that something fundamentally flawed about the world was as clear as day. It was apparent the table wanted to dismiss Timothy's agreement as being simply due to the fact that they were neighbors, but they could tell Timothy was too smart and independent for that to have been the motivation for his comment. David, who typically was relatively civil when throwing his verbal barbs, was fuming.

He snarled, "You're crazy."

Knowing David was smart enough to have meant exactly what he did in light of Timothy's subtle, yet still perceivable, mania symptoms, he decided that David had finally crossed the line, and that somebody should cut him to his own heart. It was petty, he knew, but he felt like it had been a long time coming between them, years even, and they may as well now have it out.

"Oh, that's rich coming from you. 'You're crazy' says the little man who still has to go to a therapist even though he's pushing forty."

David had never mentioned seeing a therapist, so it struck a nerve when he knew everyone saw that the comment was true. He did see a therapist. And to make it worse, anyone who knew him would say that of course he did.

"Oh, big deal. Everyone sees a therapist. There's nothing to be embarrassed about that. Only dicks think there's a problem with therapy. That's all religion is anyway, so what's the difference? You have God, I have therapy. Same thing. I'm just honest."

David's attempt to forestall the argument he knew was coming was artful. As usual, he was attempting to set up the terms of the dispute in his favor, so that when the point he knew he couldn't answer was raised, his prior pronouncement would be in place to serve as a way to deflect the conversation in whatever other direction he judged would be most to his advantage.

"Ah, yes, I see. Since you've gone ahead and equated a God-relationship and therapy, now if I say that you wouldn't need therapy if you knew God, then you can snap back and say that I wouldn't need God, if I would just accept going to therapy. You're disturbed, David, but you are clever."

Paul, who by now had lost complete track of the conversation long ago, was huddled up next to Clara, unsure about what to say. Jack was staring into his whiskey. And Mick was angry that the philosophical debate was ruining his birthday party.

He turned to Mick. "C'mon, Mick. You get to talk philosophy all day today at the lake, and that's perfectly fine, but now that I do it, I'm a big jerk? How long did you guys sit around pontificating about Buber and Leibniz today?"

Mick wanted to say that wasn't the point, that what he had done earlier was different, but he didn't say so, because he realized he wasn't upset now that they were talking philosophy, as if he would have preferred lighter fare. What bothered Mick was that the entire terms of the debate had changed. Strictly speaking, it was no longer a debate, as they understood one, since it was no longer an item of idle intellectual discussion, where everyone amused himself by seeing how his pet ideas performed against those of others. This was no longer that, no longer questioning for questioning's sake. It was about existing.

Mick was about to say something else, when suddenly the Aussie was drawn up short. They had till then all been oblivious to anything but their conversation. As if from elsewhere, the familiar riff rippling through the backyard changed that, hushing everything around them momentarily, then causing everyone to burst into wild cheering. As the thumping and pounding of synthesizers and drums reverberated through the bar's walls, shaking even the tables, including their own, the crowd started to sing along. Midnight had arrived.

The song's hypnotic melody pulsed through the yard. Even if they had still wanted to continue the discussion, it was impossible.

"It's *MGMT's* 'Kids!' I love this song!" Jack said. David got up and headed inside without looking at anyone. Mick and Jack appeared to have forgotten whatever unpleasantness there had been, and were now singing aloud, their arms draped on each other's necks, as they wiggled in their seats, dipping their shoulders.

The yard grew even more crowded, as those from inside came out to sing and dance. There was an overpowering silence, as the entire bar remained suspended in a perfect stillness, the song's slow interlude meandering its way to the final chorus, everyone's arms swaying in the air.

He locked eyes with Clara, who smiled and fluttered her eyelashes, and before she had time to register her surprise that he was not taking the open seat next to her left by Paul who had gone inside to grab her a salted iced margarita, he had plunged into the crowd, leaving her and the table behind.

He got there just as the place erupted one more time to sing in unison, the chorus repeating three times.

The euphoria which had appeared so unexpectedly, silencing the debate back at the table and throwing everyone into a whirlwind, would without doubt earn a flurry of noise complaints ensuring the end of nights like these happening here ever again. As for the conversation that had been interrupted, it suddenly seemed so trivial to him. In the heat of things, he and everyone there felt eternal, like nothing would ever end, that they would be young forever in an endless summer. The jubilation, he knew, was laced with despair, and likely so also did everyone else. This was a synthetic exuberance. This orgy of enthusiasm was destined to die on the vine. He very well would have felt completely deflated, fatigued again by the same emptiness that had consumed him earlier on the way over from the apartment. But now, things were different, and he caught a second wind, not some temporary shot in the arm, but something more approximating a rebirth, one consisting in the epiphany that everything that had happened was over, and now something new, entirely new, was at last finally here.

What he felt in looking into her eyes was different, unprecedented really, and he knew she felt what he felt also. She blushed, and her friends, two brunette twins he had never seen before, turned to look at him, having no idea who he was, but seeing that she knew him. He offered his hand, and she grabbed it. By the time they were through the crowd outside and had come out the front, he realized he'd forgotten to close out. He hadn't stopped to ask about Justice, either.

NINE

H E followed closely behind her, as she entered the park across the street. The moon was bright, and the street lights were on, so it was not dark, but in her black leather jacket, she would fade in and out, as she passed through the shadows. They reached the fountain, listening quietly for what felt like a long time, but for all he knew may have only been a few minutes.

"My name's Alison," she said.

"I know," he said.

She was genuinely surprised that he did. He, for his own part, was mystified how she could think he wouldn't have remembered her name. She was incredibly shy for such a beauty.

"People tend not to notice me," she said. It wasn't a complaint, only an observation.

"Yeah, I've noticed that."

"Noticed? Really? How would you know?" She didn't ask it accusatorily, but with veiled interest, clearly intrigued by the possibility that somebody was seeing something that had always seemed so obvious to her.

"The other night, I think it was Tuesday, when you were with—"

"Justice," she said.

"Yes, Justice." He thought she'd be impressed that he didn't avoid his name. "When you two were talking to Billy and some other people at the counter, I noticed that every time you would say something, nobody would respond. It was like you were speaking an inaudible language. I've never seen anything like it before."

"It's been that way my whole life. I don't know why it is," she sighed.

He was getting nervous, not sure where things were supposed to go. He barely knew her, but he thought he loved her, though he'd never say it, since it would sound absurd. He would have to wait, though of course he had to admit that there was no way of knowing whether there would be any such opportunity. He was speaking to a girl he'd now spoken to twice, who was already dating somebody. Simply assuming there would be another time to tell her how he felt seemed foolhardy.

He took out a cigarette. "I don't smoke," she said. He went to put the pack away in his pocket. "I want one, though," she added. He gave her the cigarette and handed her the lighter. He always thought it was clichéd to light a girl's cigarette for her. She took a drag, coughed very slightly, and then twirled around, and started walking to the park's magnolia tree.

"This one may be my favorite," he said. He could tell she entertained the idea he may have just been saying so. "Really?"

"Yeah. I live down the street, so I come here often. I like the spot." He chastised himself, mentioning his place was nearby implied more than he wanted to suggest. He felt awkward for a moment. If she took any offense or felt uncomfortable, she didn't show it. "Why do you like the tree?"

"Well, I suppose partly its association. My grandparents had a huge magnolia tree out in their front yard. I used to love climbing it with my cousin on Thanksgivings. They're easy to climb."

She started to shimmy up the trunk, and before he knew it, she was walking along a branch, as easily as a cat. "Wow, I could never do that," he said.

"Try it."

"No, no thanks."

"I thought you said you liked climbing trees."

"I said I like climbing the magnolia tree outside my grandparents' house, when I was a kid. I don't generally climb trees."

"Well, try it this time. It's fun."

"I'll watch you."

"Are you scared of heights?"

"No. I mean, not here in this case. It depends. I'm not afraid of planes, for example. And I'm not afraid of being up in a skyscraper. But I would be afraid of an open ledge, or anything exposed. I guess I'm not afraid unless I think there's a real chance of falling," he concluded. He always thought it was interesting how primal fear could be. He didn't think of himself as somebody afraid to die, but sometimes he would find his heart fluttering or a pit in his stomach, when he suddenly and unexpectedly found himself in bodily danger. Did that mean he really was afraid of death?

"Okay, well, this wouldn't be much of a fall. And I don't think you'll fall, anyway." She had a point.

Realizing that there was no way out, and that he would have to climb, he lifted his arms up, grabbed hold of a branch, swung his legs over the top of it, and dangled on the branch awkwardly, before finally twisting himself up on his stomach. He couldn't stand like she was, but eventually he was able to sit on the limb, with his hand on the trunk for added balance. He could see she wanted to laugh, but because she didn't want to offend him, she wasn't laughing.

He climbed up a few branches higher. "This is as high, as I'll go," he said.

"Perfect," she said. He thought for a second that she had just wanted to learn about him, by seeing how he would handle the challenge. His old friend from California had once told him that girls liked testing guys, that everything for them was a test, even if they didn't always necessarily know they were doing it. Of course, his friend had been single, so he felt at the time that one had to consider the source. Still, something about it seemed right. He thought that maybe she was testing him here, but if she was, it didn't feel like such a bad thing.

They jumped down to the ground. "What do you study?" he asked. He assumed she was a student.

"Studio art," she said.

"What medium?"

"Large-scale charcoal." He thought it was funny how precise she was, that she would mention it was charcoal of all things.

"Why charcoal?"

"I dunno, I just like how it looks, and it's fun to work with."

"What do you do?" she countered.

"I'm a graduate student."

"In what?"

"Philosophy," he said.

"I used to be a philosophy major. Who's your favorite philosopher?"

For a split second, he thought he'd say himself, but since he knew that would be too conceited and probably wouldn't make her laugh, he said, "Kierkegaard."

"Kierkegaard. Hm. I liked Nietzsche."

He loathed Nietzsche. Once, in a fit of passion, he had told an old teacher of his that Nietzsche was in his opinion the most overrated thinker in the history of philosophy. He realized that he had probably been overstating things when he said it, but given the worship Nietzsche received in some quarters, he did think he was a plausible candidate for among those whose thought's importance is most consistently overexaggerated.

"I hate Nietzsche," he said. Hate was perhaps too strong a word, but he wanted to make sure he was being honest with her, so he thought he'd make it clear he wasn't an admirer.

"How about Kundera?"

"Is he the one who wrote the lightness book?"

"Yes, I love that book."

"I don't really like him," again he was being honest. He hadn't read Kundera carefully, just once flipped through some pages, formed the impression he was a poetic type who basked in his sadness, and decided if he wanted to read something like that, he'd just read Nietzsche. It occurred to him that she liked Kundera, then, for the same reason he didn't, Nietzsche.

She didn't seem alarmed that so far they didn't share a taste in authors, though he could tell she was curious to see how long it might take before they found one.

"Dostoevsky?" he asked.

"Yes, I love him."

"What's your favorite novel of his?"

"*The Idiot*," she said. He worried she might think he were lying just to compensate for all the previous misses, but as it happened, that was his favorite too. "Mine, too," he said. "I've always loved the main character," he added.

"Prince Myshkin," she nodded approvingly. He wondered what it was about the Prince she liked, and of course she was right there, so he could simply ask, but asking somehow felt inappropriate. It was almost as if it were too obvious to say, as if one couldn't see it for oneself, there was no point in explaining it to anyone, because it was either self-evident or it wasn't.

"You know, apparently of all his novels, that was his personal favorite. He knew it was not in some ways his best, technically, but it had a special place in his heart." He knew for Dostoevsky personally, who believed in beauty's redemptive power, there had been something special about the task, as an artist, of depicting his image of the ideal, beautiful man. For Dostoevsky, of course, that meant depicting a Christ, a staggering undertaking, when he thought about it. He wondered why, though, if she liked Dostoevsky so much, and *The Idiot*, above all, she had a fondness for Kundera and Nietzsche.

"Do you believe in God?"

"I'm not sure," she said. "Do you?"

"Yes," he said. He was waiting for her to ask him if he were a Christian, since that question usually came next. But she didn't.

"How about Hemingway?"

"No, don't like him particularly," she answered. He knew what that must mean.

"So, you are a big Fitzgerald fan?"

"Yes! Love Fitzgerald. I don't think it's much of an argument." He agreed, but he conceded that others felt identically about Hemingway as opposed to Fitzgerald. He pointed that out.

"They're dumb," she laughed. He laughed with her too.

"Where are you from? Here?"

"No, I'm from California." He told her a bit about home.

"You?"

"Here. I like it." She paused. "But I was really supposed to go to Reed."

"Why didn't you?"

"My parents. They wanted me to stay close to home," she said.

"What do they do?"

"My mom is retired. She used to be a lawyer. My dad's a physicist at the university."

He thought about making a joke about what he and his own father thought about science dorks, but he decided he better not say anything. As an artist, she probably knew what he meant, anyway, without having to say it.

"Yours?"

"Retired. My mom used to work in computers. My dad worked in defense." Neither item seemed to interest her, so he didn't say more.

"Siblings?"

"No. You?"

"No brother. Two sisters. They died in a car crash years ago." At first, he almost laughed, because he thought she was playing a joke, but he realized she was being serious.

"I'm sorry."

"Thanks."

They were quiet again for an indeterminate time. He thought about making a comment about trees, to take them back to where the conversation started, just so it felt like there had been some coherence, or closure, and so some progress. He thought about saying something about how his favorite kind of tree might be willows.

She had walked over to the fountain and sat down, facing back to the bar. He usually never threw coins in the fountain, but he fumbled for some change, and pulled some out. He handed her a penny, which she tossed in. "You, too," she said. He flipped in a dime. He sat down beside her, but without touching. They sat in silence for a few minutes, before he gently placed his hand on her knee. She turned to him, and he looked at her. They kissed.

A car pulled up to the bar. "I have to go," she said. It wasn't him, but everyone she knew would be wanting to leave soon, so she had to go back inside. "Sandra and Stephanie will be looking for me."

"The twins?"

"Yeah, they're my best friends. What about you?"

"What do you mean?" he asked.

"Your friends. Who are they? I saw you earlier tonight sitting with a bunch of people at the table." He thought about it for a few seconds. "I don't have any friends. At least not here."

"I'll see you around. I come here a lot," she said.

"Yeah, so do I." He wanted to kiss her again, but he didn't.

She turned around and walked briskly to the sidewalk. Rusty, whom he realized now had probably seen everything, waved her in.

He came home, watched the white clovers flutter in the wind, then went to sleep.

TEN

I T was Tuesday, which this week meant meeting Carrell. Originally, the plan was to meet at one o'clock, but due to a pressing conflict to which Carrell had to attend, they were now slated to meet at three-thirty instead. At the appointed time, he saw his teacher approaching, walking over from his office to the coffee house's outdoor seating. Carrell was in his late fifties, of moderate height and fit build, with a full head of silver hair. He was dressed comfortably in matching khaki shorts and Birkenstocks. It was hot and humid, and so sweat was drenching his black shirt. Carrell tapped casually on the table.

"Need anything?" he asked, gesturing inside.

"No, thank you, I'm all set," he told Carrell.

His coffee was only half full at the moment after drinking more of it than he had intended while waiting, but it still would be enough, since his meetings with Carrell tended to be relatively brief. That would be the case again today. Despite having the heated exchange with David last Saturday night, the reading group to which they belonged was meeting at the graduate pub at four, so he would not be occupying Carrell for more than an hour. He would get through this meeting first, then deal with the awkwardness of seeing David next.

Although Carrell's demeanor was affable enough when just walking by, he knew to expect an uncomfortable discussion. James Dulas, a friend of his and once Carrell advisee himself, had left the program last year under murky circumstances. His friend's motivations were never stated explicitly. When James broke the news of his intention to leave the program, his friend had started choking up, nearly breaking down in tears. Sitting out here in the sun, only now did he see the significance that it would be at the same coffee house where he had seen James to say goodbye that he would be meeting Carrell, with his own path at a crossroads. The coffee house was the campus spot where everyone made his big decisions. When James announced his own decision to leave, he stressed how he would be glad to be returning home to Minnesota. He missed the lakes, even the snow. Clearly, he was leaving disillusioned, but he never shared the details as to why precisely. Given the circumstances, it was fair to surmise perhaps things had not ended on the best of terms with Carrell, although it was difficult to say to what extent the frayed relationship, assuming it had been so, influenced James to leave. Now, however, seeing what was happening currently with Karl, who was clashing with the program and Carrell directly, a pattern was emerging, especially if he was to count himself as the third case. From the looks of it, friction with students was not uncommon with Carrell.

In the wake, first, of James leaving and then seeing what was happening to Karl, he was seriously contemplating the idea of leaving the program too. He had not sorted out all the details yet in his mind, beyond the fact that he knew he would leave, not in order to abandon graduate school altogether, but simply to transfer. He knew nowhere is a panacea, but somewhere else could be better. He had not told Carrell yet, though he assumed that his advisor would be aware that there was a possibility he would be following James. Perhaps today was the day to mention the possibility. Yesterday, Carrell had sent him the grade for his term paper—B+. In the world of doctoral studies in which grades were a mere formality, anything below an A- was a catastrophic failure. Carrell, evidently, meant to send him a wake-up call. He lit another cigarette, as he waited.

A minute later, his advisor sauntered out, set down his latte, and took a seat. He placed his pack of cigarettes on the table within reach of Carrell—"Cigarette?"

Carrell nodded and took one, grabbed the lighter lying on the table, and lit up. This was the first time in recent memory that Carrell had accepted the offer, another indication that the conversation was shaping up to be delicate. Carrell puffed out the smoke, and looked at him.

"I read your paper, obviously. I have some additional things to say about it, but first I thought I might give you the opportunity to ask me any questions you might have."

His remark was ambiguous. It was unclear whether Carrell intended to invite him to ask something philosophically substantive about the paper material itself, or to invite a bookkeeping question about the course grade, or both.

"No," he answered.

"Well, first of all, let me emphasize, don't worry about the grade. I'll be giving you an A for the course, nonetheless." He didn't care about grades, and he knew Carrell knew that about him, so he continued to hold his tongue, waiting for Carrell to get to the point he must really be working up to making. "I thought the paper was strong, but as you'll have seen from reading my comments, I have some substantial reservations on a number of fronts." Carrell paused once again, this time for longer, expecting him to interject. He didn't know what exactly to say, and he knew there would be a more fitting opportunity to do so shortly, so he decided to still hold his peace.

Carrell continued, "One issue is strictly topical. This was supposed to be a seminar on Jaspers and Arendt. But your paper doesn't develop an argument or discussion directly pertinent to the relationship between their thought. We had talked about a number of issues throughout the course of the study that might have provided a suitable topic of analysis, but you did not pursue any of those issues themselves, or the discussions we had on them." Even though there was now more to be said in reply, this time Carrell's pause was briefer than before, and it was evident that he was neither expecting, nor desiring, a response.

"So, this has put me in a rather difficult situation as a reader, since I want to evaluate the work on its philosophical merits, but there is the expectation that the work itself would be responsive to the issues at hand covered in the independent reading." This time the pause was the most pregnant yet. Carrell took a long drag of the cigarette that was almost done, tilting his head back to exhale. He was trying to be nonchalant, but clearly the agitation had been building as he spoke.

"If you have any thoughts that you'd like to share about any of this, I'd be happy to hear them," he said, now with more than a hint of irritation in his tone.

Before settling precisely on what he would say in response, he reached for the pack on the table, and lit another cigarette.

"Sorry, want one?" he asked Carrell.

He was trying to be polite, but this time Carrell did not interpret it that way. Carrell was miffed at what he perceived to be his unnecessary stalling, and, judging by his advisor's reddening cheeks, the rage was brewing. There may be an explosion, he saw.

A scene from two years ago at the coffee shop entered his mind, a time when he was still relatively new here, but had begun to get a sense of who was who. He had been sitting outside on a sunny day just as this one, drinking coffee and smoking cigarettes with Jack and David at one of the tables. In the midst of a wide-ranging conversation on epistemology, David in the name of Kant had just ended a soliloquy declaring the end of speculative metaphysics. Jack, who was fundamentally unconvinced, asserted that, although elements of Leibniz' philosophy were perhaps no longer tenable in light of the critical philosophy, certain key elements of it remained as viable and promising as ever. David, for his part, was equally unpersuaded. As Jack was about to shift the discussion from epistemology to metaphysics instead, in order to launch into a thoroughgoing defense of how the Leibnizian doctrine of infinite analysis was itself necessary for grounding the freedom on which Kant's own practical reason's doctrine of the supreme good depends, he attempted to mediate between Jack and David. Thinking about it now, he could not recall what his specific point had been, maybe something about Heidegger. But he remembered clearly David's reaction, which at the time seemed to come entirely out of the blue, and to have had nothing to do with what he had said.

"Yeah, yeah, that's Carrell's view."

He had recognized David meant for the comment to kill two birds with one stone, on one hand, marginalizing the point itself by insinuating it was little more than a new graduate student's simply regurgitating something he had heard from somebody else, while denigrating the idea's true source, on the other. There was a startling juxtaposition in what David had said a few minutes beforehand, and what he then said next. Moments after having enlisted Kant to level an attack on the speculative metaphysics of Leibniz, David now appeared to be taking an opposite tack.

"Carrell is really just a Kantian," he said derisively.

Why criticize Carrell for that, if David were the one himself extolling Kant against Leibniz just a minute ago? David must have seen the confusion on his face, so he attempted to clarify himself. Kant, he in turn explained, was correct to rein in some of the excesses associated with the traditional metaphysical systems of, say, a Leibniz, Spinoza, or Malebranche, but a wholesale endorsement of the critical philosophy annulled too much of the post-Kantian tradition, which rightly had, since Kant's own time with the German Romanticists and German Idealists, consistently sought to lay claim to knowing things about reality that Kant's system had taken itself decisively to have foreclosed. In a word, David proposed that philosophical thought could indeed go beyond Kant, but it had at least to start with him, something Jack's endorsement of Leibniz failed to do. When David had stopped talking, and he still looked baffled as to what any of that had to do particularly with Carrell, David said sullenly, "Carrell's a jock." Coming from David, it was not a compliment. What did that mean, he wondered?

Seeing Carrell now from across the table, he finally saw what David had meant. At the time, he had discounted David's criticism of Carrell as sour grapes. But now it made sense. Carrell, who had an athletics background, championed a philosophical style that was fundamentally martial: get in somebody's face, tell him what you really think, and see what he was going to do about it. Someone like David, then, who had always resented that mentality since he was a child, because it was the same mentality that had led to him being bullied, recoiled from Carrell's philosophical persona, which to David was a continuation of a high school adolescence he found stunted.

With Carrell, it was true, there was the sense that here was a guy who was always willing to settle an intellectual dispute "off the page," if necessary. Sitting at the table listening now, he imagined himself doing something silly, like standing up on the chair and ripping his shirt off to challenge Carrell to a wrestling match, or interrupting Carrell and telling him to be quiet so they could settle things fair and square with an arm wrestle. He hadn't the slightest desire to do so, but it was fun to play out in his mind what Carrell's reaction would be if he really did something outlandish like that. Of course, it was precisely Carrell's inevitable response that revealed the irony about everything. If he did any of the things he was imagining, Carrell would naturally be mortified, or at least act as if he were, as if what was occurring was totally bizarre and unexpected. He would probably walk away in a tizzy, or maybe call campus security. The irony, of course, was that if he actually did do anything to provoke such a reaction from Carrell, whatever he did would simply be responding directly to the very fantasy everyone could see structured Carrell's professional persona. If, after all, Carrell was socially licensed to convey that the subtext of his philosophical bluntness was physical toughness, and at the same time pretend that it wasn't, when in fact that was exactly what he was doing, then why should Carrell be allowed to feign shock if somebody actually acknowledged the obvious, unspoken norm shaping all his gestures and words? In thinking about the absurdity of it all, he came to conclude that there was what was in everyone's mind, there was the world, and then there was the middle space between them, the place where everyone silently acknowledged what nobody ever said. Maybe this third space, the one outside mind and world that somehow outranked both, was itself reality—the absurd. In any case, he didn't like it, he saw why Karl and Timothy didn't like it either, and he could see how having to go through the acting with Carrell was something James before him had ultimately decided was not worth his time, either. Life was too short.

In any event, such was the undertone essential to Carrell's style that Karl, who was very intuitive, had also picked up on, and was now openly mocking Carrell over, when in email a few weeks ago he had told Carrell to "man up." Karl had shown him the exchange after he had been defending Carrell against Karl's criticisms. Karl was absolutely sure Carrell had been taunting him for months, but he was not entirely convinced by Karl's account. But the more Karl had related the details of the situation that night as they sat outside Karl's cul-de-sac apartment, the harder it was to rationalize what the program was doing to Karl. There had been certain promises made to Karl as part of his acceptance offer, those assurances were now going unfulfilled (Karl had mentioned something about funding) and now Carrell, as the department chair, was refusing to give Karl a straight answer about why those expectations were no longer going to be met. The whole experience had been immensely frustrating for Karl, who understandably was beginning to suspect that the entire reason for it was precisely that, to frustrate him. It wasn't implausible to think the people at Karl's old program at Harvard were getting those they knew here to interfere with Karl's attempt to move on.

Returning his attention to the situation directly before him at the table, he realized that whereas David had always found Carrell's style overbearing, he for his own part found it unthreatening. From what he was seeing, first with James and then Karl, and now evidently himself, it seemed Carrell was the type who lost all sense of proportion when trying to dominate somebody he sensed wasn't intimidated. He knew he certainly wasn't afraid of Carrell, just embarrassed for him, seeing now that Carrell had apparently assumed he would be.

Right as he was about to say something to Carrell that he assumed would open a long exchange of giving and asking for reasons that would be impossible to finish today before he would have to leave to meet his friends at the pub, the fuse went off. Carrell was opting for a tirade instead.

"Look," Carrell snarled gruffly, "the fact is that what you've done here in this paper is inconsistent with everything I—"

His imagination drifted to the lake. He envisioned the water lapping against his feet, and pictured the white lilies again. He thought about the ants he had seen, and the beautiful shapes the light made as it flooded through the trees on his walk to the campsite. He pictured the big clouds over the lake, and then visited again the birds in Paris. He thought about how, if he had drowned at the lake and was not able to be sitting here at the table as he was right now, Carrell would be elsewhere rather than at the coffee house, and would not care that he was dead. He didn't resent Carrell for not caring, and he didn't think Carrell was unique in the fact that he wouldn't. There was something inevitably superficial about most everyday relationships and interactions, and that was just the way it was.

It was not that he did not hear the words spewing from Carrell's mouth. He did hear them. He was even listening. It simply was that he had disconnected from them, and, being at peace knowing they did not really matter, he had no interest in letting their venom sting.

There were reasons, maybe even good ones, for why he felt as he did. To begin with, what Carrell was saying about the paper ultimately had nothing actually to do with the term paper itself. What was driving his advisor over the edge was purely personal, and it was obvious. His advisor's frustration was like his friend's father's bitterness about Manzanar, something someone said, and which was true, but it was only part of the truth, and probably not really the most important part. Beneath Carrell's wanting to grapple with another's ideas mano a mano was simply his desire to dominate the other person. The situation here at the coffee house, which was supposed to be about discussing the ideas in the paper, was really about something else. So, seeing what David saw too, he tuned Carrell out, staring at his face without saying a word, amusing himself with the thought that this must be how Carrell yells at his wife, or his kids, or the employee at the drive thru window, or his neighbor. The outward situation, as it was institutionally and socially defined, was utterly ridiculous—an old man he barely really even knew was beside himself all because of a philosophy paper he'd written.

He wondered how Alison would feel, when she learned he was thinking about leaving. He would have to tell her. He didn't want to leave now that she was here. But he didn't want to stay for this.

As for this, he was unsure how long it had been going, and when Carrell's tirade still showed no sign of abating, he noticed others at their tables were beginning to look and stare. Probably sensing that he was over the line, and was starting to embarrass himself publicly, Carrell slowly composed himself. His advisor had lost his equilibrium, and he had decided to vent his frustration with the absurdity of everything on him. Indulging his advisor's outburst wasn't hard. Frankly, it would have been cruel not to do so. They stood up, shook hands, both saying some formality about how they'd be in touch with one another soon to talk further.

He didn't mention it then, but it would be necessary to tell Carrell about the decision to transfer. The deadline for the Oxford application was soon.

Eleven

NIGHT came. The evening's twilight had been especially stunning, a majestic golden glow enshrouding the oaks and byzantine columns and archways, a chorus of cicadas providing nature's hymnal to the setting sun and the moon's ever hastening arrival. He had basked in the sun, and now he would sit under the stars, even if the city lights made them impossible to see.

He was seated at a table outside the pub, along with David and their mutual friend Goat. Everyone called him that, Goat, because he would insist on it within minutes of meeting anybody—nobody knew why he didn't go by his given name, Matthew, but complying with his bizarre name request was a small inconvenience, given the pleasure keeping his company afforded. A short, stalky man with forgettable features except for a long goatee (whatever the nickname's reason, that was not it), his appearance would be wholly unremarkable were it not for his sports jerseys and backwards baseball cap, a middle America aesthetic he enjoyed cultivating immensely, since, aside from making him the exception on a campus among academics who dressed otherwise, it also was in stark opposition to his considerable erudition, an impressive degree of learning typified above all in his mastery of no fewer than five ancient languages, including Coptic. The subject of discussion for today's session was the Synoptics, with a particular focus on Mark, but they hadn't gotten to it. After having a couple of dollar Lone Stars while waiting with Goat, David had shown up finally, frazzled from events in seminar, and, clearly no longer in any mood to have today's discussion, he had thrown his Bible on the table and said, "Well, that was the first time I read the New Testament. Won't be doing that again."

For a moment, he was sure David must be jesting. It was virtually inconceivable that a religion scholar could have advanced this far in his studies, much less his life, with this being his first time ever reading Mark. He realized, however, that David was not being facetious. Seeing the incredulity that must have been obvious on his face, David shot him a contemptuous look. He could tell by the expression that David was already plotting his revenge to strike at some point later in the conversation tonight. He sighed. The argument from Saturday at the bar was not yet put away.

The ensuing discussion, perhaps surprisingly, had remained lighthearted and even jovial, mostly consisting of wisecracks and harmless anecdotes and other observations about everyday things. Goat and he talked sports. David reminisced about a beloved cabin in Canada. Others they knew had been joining them until they had to pull up a second table. It appeared that the attack from David he was expecting would perhaps not come.

Goat stood up. "You want one?"

"Yes," he said, fishing three dollars from his pocket. He owed Goat for the one before.

"Thanks." Goat took a bill from David also, and shuffled into the bar, which lay tucked away down on the basement level only accessible through a discreet staircase beneath the biology building. At the tables, two doctoral students from the religion program, and a third from history, were talking about the Book of Baruch at the table. "It's narrative among Jewish apocalyptic literature is unusual in that . . . " one of them was saying. He was briefly distracted as Goat returned with the beer.

"Here you go. Cheers," Goat said.

They all took sips. As he was about to turn his attention back to the conversation, his gaze was drawn to a solitary young man standing next to one of the courtyard's nearby oaks. Without saying a word or offering any greeting, the man, who appeared to be in his late twenties, probably a fellow graduate student, though it was difficult to tell from which department, maybe engineering judging by his beard, sauntered over, and stood over his left shoulder, right between Goat and him.

"Consciousness isn't merely a neurochemical process," the man said.

At first, he thought the man might be addressing somebody else at the table, perhaps commenting on something from a discussion earlier that night, but when the rest of the table continued talking about Baruch without paying him any notice, he realized that the man must be addressing him. He glanced at Goat, who was looking straight ahead at David, both of whom seemed to be engrossed in the conversation. He wracked his mind, struggling to identify who this is and where they must have met, but he couldn't remember, not even a name. Evidently the man knew who he was, because he didn't introduce himself, but proceeded on familiar terms. Standing still, he continued, "I'm sure you've wanted to understand. The problem is that for too long researchers have been investigating within a framework that renders answers impossible." Earlier in the evening, shortly after David had arrived, the group had talked about the possible origins of consciousness, but it was a matter that had remained the subject of discussion for only a few passing minutes, and it was something that the man would not have heard—he didn't remember seeing him at the pub then. For a moment, he wondered whether the man had been present at some other conversation at which the topic had come up, maybe at a seminar or a lecture or a party, but still, he couldn't recall his face. By now the man had been talking long enough that it was too late to ask his name, because the man, whoever he was, would assume that he remembered who he is.

He tried focusing less on the fact that he couldn't place the man, and more on what he was saying. "Descartes, as you know, had speculated it's the pineal gland that houses the key to the union between mind and body. For a long time, people mocked the idea, dismissing it as baseless speculation on his part, but he was right. It's a mystery as to how he could have known, since at the time, the science was not sufficiently advanced to have suggested the hypothesis to him. He must have deduced it on metaphysical considerations alone, or maybe even mystical ones," the man said.

"Yes, right. There's that story I heard about Descartes claiming to have been visited by an angel once. He said something about it in a letter somewhere, I think," he said to the man.

"Correct. He was given a revelation of the inner workings of nature," the man said, looking directly at him with a smile and twinkle in his eye.

Though he wasn't directly party to the conversation, Goat shifted uncomfortably in his chair, coughed nervously as if to clear his throat, and then chugged down the rest of his Lone Star. He crushed the plastic cup, tossing it into the nearby basket: "And it's good!" he hooted. Goat and he locked eyes for a brief moment as the visitor continued.

"But enough about Descartes. The point is that modern science still did not have the capability of unraveling the mystery of consciousness. Consciousness is not a purely materialistic process, so it's impossible to understand it by means of physics, or biology, or chemistry alone." He thought this might be a natural place at which to ask the man what he studied, since presumably he worked in one of the science labs on campus.

"Which department are you?" he asked.

"I'm not with the university," the man replied.

He felt like asking why, then, somebody who wasn't a student or teacher at the university would be at the campus pub, why he would want to talk about consciousness of all things, why he would come to this table rather than any of the others, and from where they knew each other, if not from here at school. But before he had the chance to get a sentence out, the young man was saying more.

"The key lies in biophysics. The field is young but promising, you'll see."

"How so?" he asked.

"It understands that there is no way to explain the interactions between the brain and the mind, nature and consciousness, with the current models we have been using," he said.

He was preparing to say something about scientific reductionism and the relation between physics and biology, but before he could, the young man stared straight at him, and with a complete assurance that his words would be understood, said, "But you know what I'm trying to say. You think about it a lot, and have been for years. Listen to me: biophysics. Only it can comprehend the wraith."

"The wraith?"

The young man smiled knowingly, and without saying another word, nodded and walked away. He waited a few minutes to see whether the man would return, since perhaps he had gone into the bar to grab a beer or use the restroom. When it was clear he had vanished, he turned to the rest of the table.

"Hey, guys, who was that?" he asked everyone.

They all paused, and looked confused. "Who?"

"Uh, the guy that just left."

"What guy?"

He was now even more confused. He gestured in the direction to which the man had disappeared. "The one that was standing right next to me for the last five or ten minutes talking about consciousness."

Nobody knew of whom he was talking. He had assumed they'd been listening to some of what the man had said. At the very least, they would have seen him standing at the table. A passage from Simone Weil, which he had not recalled in years, suddenly stirred within him. And though he did not say it aloud, he quietly mouthed the words, "Chance—for I always prefer saying chance rather than Providence—made of him a messenger to me."

He appealed to Goat, "I thought he knew somebody here. You don't know who he was?" he asked.

With a face white as a sheet, Goat said uneasily, "No, I thought you knew who he was."

"Did you catch his name?" he asked Goat, double-checking to make sure he hadn't somehow missed it.

"No, he never said anything."

Neither of them said another word, because they both knew they didn't have to. True, the visitor had felt relatively benign. But his discreet apparition, which had taken the form of an inexplicable and unbidden intrusion, had been eerie nonetheless. They took some comfort in the popular truism that there is no such thing as ghosts.

Twelve

I   T was nearly nine, which was still early, but he was tired. He thought about walking home. Before he stood to leave, his phone vibrated. It was a local friend of his, a law student, whom he originally had met at one of the coffee shops nearby his apartment. They would study together sometimes, and now they were becoming drinking buddies too.

"Drink?" it said. His friend must be finishing studying at the coffee shop, meaning he would be nearby the bar.

"Sounds good," he said.

"Cool, I'll be there at ten," the reply read.

Without saying so, they knew which spot they had in mind, the same place he had been at Saturday and Tuesday. He thought about the magnolia tree.

With the new plans meaning he was no longer going straight home, he could not use being tired as an excuse to leave. He generally avoided lying, especially about small things, since he felt there was something particularly sinister in choosing to lie over a triviality whose truth was relatively painless, so he decided to tell everyone that he was leaving for elsewhere. Maybe someone would want to join him. He told them.

"Sorry, can't go. I should be heading out anyway. Jessica already wants me home," Goat said.

Goat was the only one married. It was another fact that contributed to his middle American persona.

"I swear, sometimes I think that's the only reason you ever got married, Goat, just to be able to constantly remind everyone that you are," David quipped.

The others at the table did not know him well, so naturally they were uninterested in accepting the offer. That left David as the only remaining potential taker.

"I parked off campus," David continued, switching his attention from Goat to him, "but we could walk over to my car and drive. I don't want to leave it here, if I'm going to the bar."

David was going, then. He was pleased to hear it, since having the opportunity to spend time alone together might clear the air, and help dispel the lingering animosity from Saturday.

"Okay, great. Ready when you are," he said. Everyone stood to say their goodbyes.

Out of the corner of his eye, he saw the pub door swing open and clang against a railing. Everyone startled and looked over. Mick was approaching. He had been drinking heavily, and was wobbling as he made his way to the tables. His eyes were nearly shut, and his jaw was dangling open—it appeared he may even start drooling. He stumbled over, and plopped on a chair, which, tilting into a crack it caught on the courtyard, almost sent him spilling off the chair onto the ground. He braced himself with his arm, palm to the ground, just in time. Embarrassed to see him like this, everyone but David and Goat left hastily.

When the others were out of earshot, Goat leaned in and said, "Mick, are you okay, buddy? What are you doing? This is really bad."

The Aussie didn't seem to hear.

"Mick, it's David. Do you know where you are?" David appeared to be amused by the spectacle, although he was going to do what he could to help.

"Mick," he said, placing his hand on Mick's shoulder, "You need to go home now. David was just about to leave here. He can drive you home." Goat looked at David expectantly.

"Yes, that's right you ol' sad sack, I can take you home." Despite being detached from Mick's plight, David perceived the situation for what it was, seeing that this excess wasn't driven by enthusiasm, like Saturdays after the lake, but rather by despair.

"Shut up you, guys. It's not funny," Mick slurred.

"Nobody's laughing at you, Mick," Goat said.

"That's not true. I am. But it's okay, it's fine, Mick. We'll get you home," David said.

Before they could help him to his feet, Mick stood up, and careened into the main oak in the courtyard. He leaned his forearm against the trunk, his head in his hand. They looked away when they realized he was urinating.

"Oh, God," Goat said. David was laughing hysterically. "Attaboy, Mick!"

"It's not funny, David. The police could arrest him. What if his teachers see?" Goat said.

Mick finished, walked over, and slumped down at the table. "Take him and get him out of here, guys," Goat said. They all helped him to his feet, and told him they were taking him to the car, so he could go home.

The silver Oldsmobile was parked a block from campus, just down the street from Karl's cul-de-sac. David brushed off some leaves that had fallen on the hood. For a moment, he silently considered whether they should stop at Karl's to surprise him. "Karl won't want to go," David said, having also considered the possibility himself.

They got in, and rolled their windows down. David lit a cigarette. The car's wheels, which had been turned toward the curb, drove up on the curb as David pulled away. "Bah," he said, as the car thumped down back onto the street. Mick was on the verge of vomiting, as he laid sprawled out delirious in the back seat. They drove a few blocks to Mick's, where a roommate, Rose, was waiting to help him in. "Thanks," she said, as she helped Mick out of the backseat.

"Have a good night, mate," David chuckled as the door shut.

They sat parked in front, while David lit a cigarette. He did too. "What was that all about, do you think?"

"Who knows. I'll find out later," David said. He pulled out, and they were silent for a minute, as he drove on.

"How's your dissertation going?" he asked.

"Terrible. It's garbage, but my advisor told me not to worry. At this point it's just about finishing," David said.

"I'm sure it's good," he said.

He was being sincere. If his writing was even halfway adequate, he found it hard to believe the dissertation could be that bad, given how sharp David was. David was apparently being modest. Sometimes he would be self-deprecatory to invite praise, but not this time.

"Well, I don't need anyone's support with it. I'm fine," David said icily.

He thought about why David would resent anything he had just said about the dissertation. Then it occurred to him that mentioning it must have led David to infer he meant to be bringing up Saturday's events, where everyone had been talking about Buber. He hadn't intended his comment about the dissertation to invite a larger conversation about Saturday. Clearly David didn't want to talk about it, and neither did he, but if he mentioned that now, it would appear he was saying so to agree with David only after his attempt to broach the subject had been rebuffed. He looked out the window, and wondered how much of everyone else's lives were besought with these little confusions and miscommunications that piled up. Before they were forced to settle on what next to talk about instead, they reached the bar and parked the car.

Rusty was working the door. "Hi, guys," he said, as they came up the stairs. He shook their hands and was glad to see them, despite a hint of surprise on his face from seeing them walking in together. Rusty, who had been working the door on Saturday, probably had seen David and the others leave that night at closing time. Whatever they had said about him and the events from earlier that night would not have been flattering. He thought about how strange a job it must be, to sit and observe everyone's lives like a fly on the wall, watching the fallout, and everyone's clumsy ways of trying to work through whatever it was that resulted. Having unfettered access to what people were concealing from others gave Rusty something like an omniscient perspective. And while he was not the type who would ever ask Rusty about what others had said about him, he tried to imagine what Rusty was making of the situation.

When they walked inside, there were a few people seated at the counter. They could hear voices on the balcony upstairs, but the booths were all empty.

"Booth?" he asked.

"No, bar," David said.

Billy was working. "The usual?"

"Yes, please," he said.

Billy went to the fridge, grabbed two Lone Stars, popped the caps off, poured two whiskeys, and set the drinks down on the counter.

"Four dollars," he said.

He saw David begin reaching for his wallet. "David, don't worry about it. I got it." He already had the bills out, but David insisted.

"It's cheap. I can take care of it," David said. He thought about clarifying that he hadn't been insinuating David couldn't afford it, but like before with the confusion over the dissertation in the car, he decided to let it be.

It was then that he realized the revenge he had anticipated at the graduate pub but had failed to materialize was coming now. David had been storing up his wrath, saving it for later, probably because he didn't want the others to see it. Now that they weren't on campus, David said, "I don't expect you to apologize for how you behaved on Saturday, frankly I don't need you to do that, but I did want to say that it upset me, it upset others, and you should be aware that your actions have consequences. I'm pretty thick-skinned, but not everybody else is."

He thought about where he would begin, if he were inclined to point out all that was wrong about that statement. He would observe that if he should apologize, so should David; he would observe that if David really wasn't expecting an apology there was no reason to bring up the fact he wasn't looking for one; he would observe that if David were upset, so was he; he would observe that he didn't deny his actions have consequences, so it was patronizing and arrogant to suggest he had to be reminded that they did; he would observe that it was disingenuous to speak for others when they weren't here to speak for themselves; and, above all, he would observe that if David were anything, it certainly wasn't thick-skinned, a fact manifest by the way he was currently ambushing him over something that by now wasn't any longer worth discussing. Instead, like at the coffee house with Carrell, he let the other play out the fantasy. David wanted him to say everything he just thought to himself, so that he could entangle them both in a knot impossible to untie, but because he didn't want to involve himself in it, he kept silent.

David chuckled when he perceived that he wasn't taking the bait. "You think you're so smarter than everyone else," David said. Another provocation. He wouldn't note that the same could be said of David, and so he shouldn't project, or that David presumed to know so much about his heart, when David was the same one that constantly told everyone that it was wrong to judge others.

Realizing that this second provocation was no more effective than the first, David paused to recalibrate. "Cigarette?" he suggested.

If he said no, he knew David would take that as a minor victory, a sign that, although he had been able not to say anything escalating the situation, he had succumbed to the temptation of reflexive noncompliance the moment he had seen the chance. It didn't matter, of course, that there was simply the possibility that he didn't want to smoke, David would refuse to consider it, so rather than feed in to his interpretation, he surprised David.

"Sure, sounds good."

He walked to the cigarette machine by the pool table, bought a pack of cigarettes, glanced over at the photo booth in the corner, and walked back to the counter. "Downstairs or upstairs?" he asked David.

If David wanted to pretend that he was being difficult, then he would defer to David in everything, even if it became comical, since that, he supposed, would serve its own purpose. The entire situation was ridiculous, after all, and he knew David knew it too.

"Ah, I see, letting me make all the decisions. Very nice of you," David snickered. David wanted him to reply that it had been his intention to be obvious, so of course David saw, but again, he bit his tongue, and stepped over the trap.

"I don't know what you'd do without me, David. You wouldn't be able to amuse yourself," he said instead.

"Kinda like how I don't know what you'd do without God," David shot back. "You're too smart for that," David added.

He felt good that he'd worked through the preliminaries, by avoiding the warm-up provocations, so that they could get on with the main issue. Here they were.

"Downstairs?" he asked, as they got to the stairs.

"Yeah," David said.

He opened the patio door, strode out, and grabbed a stool at the railing near the sidewalk where he liked to sun himself in the afternoons. He looked up. The stars were invisible, but the moon was full, without a cloud in the sky.

Noticing the moon too, David said, "Ah, I long for the times when we thought the moon was near, as it appears, and that the sun moved over the face of the earth. The truth is ugly." Rather than take David's allusion to Nietzsche as his point of reference, in reply, he decided he would have David answer Kierkegaard.

"You've read Kierkegaard, David."

"Yes, of course. Brilliant, but ultimately deluded," he stated.

"You psychologize everything," he stated, the reference to their weekend argument about therapy being deliberate.

"What else is there?" David retorted.

"Well, as you know, were that all there is, there would be no point in arguing about anything, much less everything, since all there would be are interpretations. But since all you like to do is argue constantly about everything, I have to conclude you're being dishonest with yourself, and, contrary to what you always say, you do think there's more to existence than interpretations. Then again, maybe you're angry, because you can't stop from arguing even though you recognize it's pointless doing so, if you're really right."

"I don't have any problem accepting things are interpretation. Nietzsche was absolutely right when he said it's all interpretation. Maybe everything's an illusion. So be it," he said.

He could run through the logic from last Tuesday when, here alone at the bar, he had considered whether everything is an illusion, and how, if so, that would lead to a contradiction. He remembered how he had come to the conclusion that it was an argument he had had too many times already, one he was tired of having, and one that in a way didn't make sense to him anymore, since it didn't change anybody's mind. He felt he was right about that; it was an empty argument. So rather than arguing to David about how nihilism can't be true if everything is indeed an illusion, he said nothing.

There was something about his silence that offended David. "You always stop arguing when you think it will make the point for you, that somehow you're showing everyone you're right, by no longer trying to convince them that you are. That's dishonest, I think," David said.

"I think you provoke people endlessly, because that's all that gives you temporary relief from whatever's really bothering you," he said.

"Yes, well, that's what I've been trying to figure out at therapy. You avoid the question by pretending you have all the answers," he stated. "God is the lazy way out," he added, as if what he had meant wasn't already clear.

"Shouldn't you say the coward's way out? Nietzsche is all about strength."

"There is such a thing as intellectual courage, obviously. Believing the truth can require bravery. But, anyway, whether you want to call it cowardice or laziness, the point is that belief in God is what it is," said David.

"Well, I just find it interesting that you of all people are the one making the martial metaphors, insinuating that it's strength and courage that decide who does or doesn't believe the truth, when you're the one who so often criticizes people like Carrell for being a jock about ideas."

For a moment, David didn't know what to say. David knew he knew David had complete disdain for Carrell for that reason, and David realized that he was adopting a stance toward the issue that was reminiscent of the very mentality he'd typically mock as infantile. He had noticed this before, how as much as atheists are united in their dislike for God or the belief in God, they always had such contempt for each other at the same time, and were always bickering about everything else. The best way to show the instability in an atheist's own position was to point out its parallel to some-body else whose thinking and personality he couldn't stand.

"Well, I don't want to get into him," David said. "If I ever said he was a jock, what I meant is that he wants disciples. Especially in his students."

He had a question he would like to ask Carrell, whom he assumed was an atheist too. So he asked David. "Why do you harp on God so much, if you think he doesn't exist?"

"I'm not angry at God. I'm angry at—well, I wouldn't say angry—I don't respect people who live a lie thinking there's a God," he said.

"Yes, but you're the one who said that things are all an illusion. If be-lieving in God is one illusion among others, why is that the one that bothers you so much? You're going to tell me that's a coincidence?"

"It's an illusion that those who believe shove in other people's faces, and it's obnoxious. And the delusion only worsens, too, as people get older." The implication was that, given that he was already a believer now, he'd be unimaginably intolerable when he was older.

He thought David was right that many people probably do become increasingly fervent in their faith as they age. But he didn't see the objection to it. "I suppose many people who reject God when they're young, only get more rabid in their hatred of God as they got older. Same thing. There's only two directions, and everyone chooses one."

"Uh, oh please," David sighed. "You're too smart for that. Everything's always so binary with you."

"Maybe the truth is simple," he said.

"Christ, you're an idiot sometimes," David laughed.

It took all his strength not to criticize David for the blasphemy. Once again, it was David taunting him. He felt like they were going in circles, and that the conversation was futile. The scorecard was fairly easy to keep. David thought he was weak for believing in God; he thought David was weak for not believing. David thought he was delusional for thinking he saw something that was only a phantom; he thought David was delusional for blinding himself to what he'd otherwise see if he hadn't. David thought he sought happiness in a comforting lie; he thought David preferred his misery if it meant not having to accept the truth made demands of him that he was unwilling to accept.

Although he knew it was entering only in fragmented form, he could recall the majority of the passage from memory that seemed to him relevant, "It was as if an error slipped into an author's writing and the error became conscious of itself as an error . . . and now this error wants to mutiny against the author, out of hatred toward him, forbidding him to correct it and in maniacal defiance saying to him: No, I refuse to be erased; I will stand as a witness against you, a witness that you are a second-rate author." Disbelief was defiance, he thought.

As if reading his mind, David said, "You want to be appeased. That's your mistake."

"The trouble is that you don't. You want to believe the truth can't be beautiful. You say that's naïve, because you're scared of what it would mean for you if it were true. So you writhe in your self-imposed disaffection."

"Oh, Jesus. Give me a break," he said.

As he studied David, he could see that David thought resorting to breezy blasphemy had power in it, like it somehow proved the name could not signify anything it was said to mean, because if it did, there would be no way a man, any man, could just casually defy God by taking the name in vain. A truly powerful God would not allow his creatures to do that, but his creatures can, *ergo* there must not be any such God. Thinking there was proved to be superstition. He saw that for David, blasphemy was like performing an exorcism, but instead of chasing away evil, it kept at arm's length the idea there was a God who cared. He knew that if he tried mentioning to David how he had once read in a biography of Dostoevsky how the latter's friends loved mocking Christ viciously in order to drive him to tears, he would misunderstand his statement. David would construe his comment as intending to equate himself with Dostoevsky. He would be accused of arrogance and laughed at, and the point he had hoped to make by mentioning it would go unaddressed. There is nothing new under the sun—that is what he wished to say by it. But rather than explain why he, just like others before him, derive such immense delight in mocking Christ, David would choose to turn the subject to anything else, and, in this case, that would mean channeling his scorn directly on him for what he said, without addressing it squarely. He said nothing.

His mind produced the scene of the time when he was ten years old, and his father was working on the ladder fixing an issue with the garage roof. He had been standing at the foot of the ladder watching the work. He could no longer remember what exactly it was, but something had gone wrong, maybe his father had dropped a tool, so he said under his breath loudly enough for his father to hear, "Jesus." His father snapped around immediately, and through a clenched jaw he had never seen before, said, "What did you just say? Don't ever say that again." He had never seen his father so stern, and he felt fear and shame for what he had done to cause it, though he wasn't sure what exactly that had been. He didn't understand what he had said. The only reason he said it was because he had heard his grandfather say it before when he was frustrated. He knew his father was a good man, and he trusted him, so he knew that there must be a good reason for his father's being upset. But he also had thought his grandfather was a good man, too, so he was confused why, then, his grandfather would have said what he had, if his father thought it such a bad thing to say. He tried understanding what possibly could be explaining the disagreement between them, but eventually he dropped it, when he couldn't make sense of it. Only now, years later on this muggy Texas night, had he thought about that moment.

A voice other than David's interrupted his revery. "Hey, buddy."

It was his friend, the law student from the coffee shop, walking up the stairs. Rusty waved him through. Jackson Nowak was a gregarious man of twenty-six, ambitious and slightly arrogant, but generally good-natured and well-intentioned. He liked disappointing people's stereotypes of him, which is why he maintained his hair in an overly-gelled, slicked-back style. Even though he knew in the real world it proved a sham, Jackson liked to pretend that the legal profession was noble, that ethics came first, and that he was destined to be wealthy and successful the honest way. The certitude he would become so, and with the utmost integrity, was partly what lent to the inevitable impression he was a little too self-confident, but he personally could look past Jackson's egoism, when it was to a large extent rooted in a sincere belief that he was capable of not having to compromise his integrity in the way others thought necessary.

A minute after barging through the front door, Jackson emerged on the patio, three shots in hand. "It's shot time, guys," Jackson said.

"Thanks, man," he said.

"No thanks, I should be going. It's a Tuesday, so tonight's not the night for this," David said. He left the porch without saying a word, walked out the front door, and waved faintly to them down the stairs without looking. The headlights to the Oldsmobile came on, and the car puttered down to the light, where it made a left, and disappeared from view behind the repair shop.

"What was that guy's problem? What a dick," Jackson laughed. He put on a serious face. "Sorry, he's your friend?"

"Yeah, he's someone I know from school." He was about to say more, but Jackson's comment gave him a bit of distance from the situation. It was like a dark cloud dispersing, and he decided to let it go.

They spent a couple hours chatting pleasantly about law school and some girl Jackson was interested in. When it reached midnight, he felt like it was time to go home. Jackson knew it was a short walk for him to the apartment, but because it looked like there was still something on his mind that his friend wanted to say, Jackson offered to drive him home the short distance. When they got there, he idled the car outside the entryway to the main courtyard. As he was about to close the passenger door, he heard Jackson lean over the center console. With a serious face, Jackson said, "Hey man, look at the moon." He looked up, and then back to Jackson. Jackson was quiet for a few seconds.

"The moon is not for you, it just is," he said. He laughed to himself, said goodbye, and drove off.

He understood Jackson's point, which he recognized had some truth to it. Ultimately, though, he disagreed, even if he couldn't say why exactly. If she were here, she would know. But there was no way to reach her.

Thirteen

T HE next morning, he went out for a cigarette in the courtyard. There was no shade at the table, but the sun felt good, the warmth of which would help him emerge from the grogginess. He sat and watched the birds hopping in the grass. The clovers were still there, having withstood a storm that must have blown in during the night when he was sleeping.

He contemplated everything that had changed in a week. Or, if not changed, at least come more into focus, he decided. Karl, who was supposed to show up at Mick's birthday party, had not shown up, his sudden reclusiveness portending a permanent departure, both from the philosophy program and the city. Timothy, who on Saturday night had appeared to be in the best shape in recent memory, hadn't been seen at the apartment since, which suggested he was either at the hospital going through the motions, or he had gone off the deep end finally, and taken a trip to conceivably anywhere. As for Mick, things had inexplicably taken a turn for the worse, when last night he looked utterly disconsolate after having been in such good spirits over the weekend. Jack, who had no plans to leave like Karl or Timothy, would be clinging on to old habits, even if they were starting to catch up with him, if his persistent cough were any indication. Tony, who at this stage was probably the most stable of everyone, was increasingly having less in common with them, and it would not be surprising if he went home to Miami to start anew. Paul was descending into an even worse alcoholism, and it likely wouldn't be long before Clara lost patience and left him because of it. Where she would go when everyone else started to leave was unclear. David, who was always sensitive to the situation around him, must have sensed that what had been everyone's routine for the last couple of years was now rapidly disintegrating, and that it was time to finish his thesis and leave for Canada. And then there was Cody, who, eagerly awaiting his acceptances from doctoral programs, was displaying an obvious distaste for everything here, which was becoming clearer each time he showed up. Thus, sensing that this would be the last summer everyone would be together, David and Jack were throwing a party at their apartment on Saturday night, the pretext being Jack's fortieth birthday. Everyone would be there.

As he lit another cigarette, he watched the squirrels scamper along the branches of the courtyard's elm tree. Laplacian determinism could not account for something so simple, he thought. Even the squirrels have an integrity all their own, their irreducible style of being indicating that they were far more than an assemblage of atoms. In the name of science, metaphysical reductionism merely eliminated nature, rather than explained it. In principle, he could concede somebody like David having a genuine hesitation over whether a man had a soul, or whether instead humans were simply animals. But he had no comprehension of how others like Cody or Tony could seriously maintain that living creatures like these squirrels playing here in the tree were an illusion, just complicated arrangements of an underlying biological and physical complexity leaving no room for things such as humans, squirrels, and trees. It was all atoms and the void to them. A squirrel with a nut wandered up to the table. It went about its business unconcerned with him. He laughed to himself and shook his head.

He stood to head inside, realizing the train of thought he'd just had no longer held the sway over him it once would have. For so long, he had been able to talk endlessly about such matters, with anyone at any time, very often late into the early morning hours, whether at people's apartments or houses, in the car on long drives, at bars, in seminar rooms, or discussion and reading groups. It was one ever-expanding, never-ending conversation about everything that now felt empty. The idea of heading over to the coffee house where Jackson and the philosophy students would be at this hour was inconceivable, the prospect of listening to them arguing about whether a squirrel possessed more than a material cause, but formal and final ones also, was revolting to him. If he were being honest, he didn't care anymore whether Aristotle, or Newton, or Kuhn was right about the nature of squirrels. It didn't make sense to him how such a question, even assuming there was any way of answering it decisively, had anything to do with what mattered. He was tired of life being one long argument, or series of them.

His memory dredged up an encounter from the previous fall. He, Goat, David, and another doctoral student, a man in his late forties who was already something of a burgeoning icon in the world of psychonautics, were all sitting on the front porch of a yuppie bar. David and the other went inside for a pitcher, and he went to light a cigarette.

"You should quit those, you know," Goat said.

"Yeah, I know," he said, assuming an acknowledgment would suffice to halt the conversation.

Goat, however, pressed on with his admonishment. "When you smoke, people see why, they know it's because you're tormented. Only unhappy people smoke," he said. For a fleeting moment, he thought about pointing out that only sad people drink the way they all do, including Goat himself, but he was silent. Goat was right about the cigarettes, he knew.

Seeing his comment had hit the mark, Goat concluded with a word of encouragement. Gesturing inside to where David and their psychonaut friend had just entered, he said, "Don't become like those two." Goat paused, adjusted his hat, and opened the Bible to the reading selection which that day had been the Epistle of James. "We're not like them," Goat concluded, looking up at him from the book.

As the image of the scene from memory faded but the mood it evoked did not, his attention returned to the room around him. He looked over at the shelf, grabbed a book off it, walked out the door, and stepped into the courtyard. For a moment, he almost decided to head over to the coffee house, after all, but he overrode the force of habit with an act of will in the name of something he couldn't quite put into words. Heading right rather than left, he walked up the street and in short order was at the park. The fountain was flowing, and he took a seat at a bench by the magnolia, the Millrose Tower casting its shadow onto the secluded plaza. He could not explain why, but he felt like Alison should be here too, or that she would be soon. He waited a while, and then sighed and stood. Over at the bar, which had just opened, Rusty was putting out a chair, as he was evidently working the afternoon shift today. He must have felt somebody watching him, because he looked up, stared into the park, and then waved. Seeing Rusty, he decided he may as well stop in.

"Hey, Rusty," he said at the top of the stairs.

"Hey, buddy, great to see you," Rusty said. The smile was big and genuine. They shook hands, and they paused, seeing whether the other would say anything first, but when neither of them did, they broke out laughing together. There was no reason to say anything, because there was too much to say if they tried, and anyway they both already knew what there was to say, so there was no reason to bother saying it. He admired that about Rusty, that Rusty was comfortable not having to say something always, that he understood a silence could communicate as much as anything, sometimes even more than words.

His mind drifted to an old friend of his in California, Justin Reinman, who was just that way. They could go hours without saying a word to one another, because they knew there was nothing to say. It has been a few years since they had spoken, but it felt like a pause, a long silence that he knew his friend also knew would be overcome whenever they decided to pick up the conversation again. He realized he probably didn't think enough about Justin, because it reminded him of their mutual friend, the same friend who'd told him about the world of blackmail and corporate espionage. When their friend committed suicide not too long ago, there were now no more stories about Portland restaurants or anything else. Avoiding Justin, he realized, was a way of not having to remember their friend's death. He thought that Justin probably understood this, or that he would have found a reason to justify his silence, anyway. He realized that was what made him a true friend, as opposed to the people here now in his life. No matter what he did, with them, it was never enough, and there was always something wrong, something they were upset with him for having done or not having done. But with Justin, it was the opposite. He couldn't think of a single time they'd ever so much as shouted at one another.

He took a seat at the bar, and was about to take out his phone to call his friend in California, when Billy came over. "The usual?"

"No, thanks. Lemonade, please."

"Sure thing," Billy said. He poured him a glass, and set it down. "On the house."

He walked out to his spot on the front patio for a cigarette. He lit it, and stuck his head out over the railing into the sunshine. "Yeah, boy, that's nice, isn't it?" Rusty said. The door behind him on the patio opened, there were some footsteps, and the sound of somebody pulling up a stool next to his.

"Gentlemen," the young man said. "Think I might join you myself. Sunning like a couple of cats looks pretty good," the man added.

Lofton, he did not know his last name, was a regular at the bar, somebody with whom he would chat during afternoons like these. He had very light blond hair, just like Timothy's, only it was cut short. Most of the time he had on a smile like a Smurf, which only drew attention to his pale blue eyes, which were incredibly kind, but also deeply sad looking. Lofton worked as a waiter at a nearby restaurant. After using his paycheck to pay the rent, he would use his tips to come here, nursing a severe drinking problem suggesting a melancholy whose cause was too sensitive for anyone to ask about. Nothing was determinate, but the sadness had the aura of the death of a loved one. He would walk everywhere, including here to the bar, having lost his license after a recent DUI. It was only recently that the two had learned they were neighbors, Lofton's own complex, The Oaks, lying just a stone's throw from his, the two apartments sharing a fence. They had been making plans to meet up somewhere rather than here, but it never happened, since, on occasions like this one today, they found themselves together on the patio, with nowhere else to be. He realized that, like Justin and Rusty, Lofton was somebody who said relatively little, because he had too much to say. For a few minutes, the three of them sat in silence, smiling in the sun, enjoying each other's presence.

"Excuse me guys, I'll be right back," he said to them.

He went in, walked over to the cigarette machine to buy some more, then walked down the checkerboard hallway to the bathroom. On the way back to the patio, he stopped at the bar for another lemonade, then stepped outside. As he descended the stairs and was about to round the corner, he could hear voices besides Lofton's. "There he is," Lofton said pointing to him.

Alison was smiling, sitting casually in a white blouse and brown skirt. For a split second he worried he might drop his glass from surprise.

"Oh, uh, hi," he stammered.

He didn't want to appear rude, but he was afraid to be overly familiar. Aside from the usual nervousness that might be expected, there was the further fact that she was with the twins, the two of them sitting on opposite shoulders.

"Hi," he said introducing himself to them. Neither of them was eager to talk, and he could tell they were suspicious since Alison clearly lit up when she saw him, but with Lofton being there, they could not do much about it. They were stuck.

"Do you know Lofton?" he asked the twins.

"Yeah. We've seen him here," Sandra said as if distractedly.

Lofton seemed not to notice, or perhaps not to care. "Well, since it's turning out to be something of a gathering, how about we all go get some shots?" Lofton suggested.

The twins noticeably perked up.

"I'll need someone to help," Lofton continued. Alison stood up intending to go. She waited for Lofton to reach the stairs, and then she made her way too, her hand almost brushing up against his leg, as he watched her try catching up to Lofton, who was a few feet ahead of her, waiting on the stairs. He could feel Sandra watching them like a hawk.

It was silent for a minute on the patio. The twins were on their phones, and occasionally they would look up to say something to one another about their text conversations. Sandra set her phone next to her Strongbow on the railing, put her hand under her chin, her elbow on the counter, and turned to him. "So, who are you?"

He had already told her his name, so he said, "I live in the neighborhood."

"Yeah, that makes sense, since you're here in the afternoon. What do you do?"

"I'm a graduate student," he said, taking care not to refer to himself as a philosopher. She didn't ask what he studied.

"You know Alison?" Stephanie asked. The question was searching, but not quite as pointed as Sandra's tone of questioning. He judged that Stephanie must be the happy twin.

"Yes. Well, not really. We've met," he said. "Actually, we met here last week," he added.

"Cool," she said, though it was clear she was still deciding what to think of him and the situation.

"What do you do?" he asked. He was asking both of them, but Sandra pretended he was only asking Stephanie.

"Well, I'm not sure how it will go, but right now I'm thinking of becoming a flight attendant," Stephanie said.

"Oh, that would be really cool," he said. "Don't you get discounts?" he asked.

"Yeah, attendants get free personal travel," she said. He was contemplating asking where should we be travelling, but he could tell that Sandra thought he was the type who would only ask such a thing because he hadn't travelled himself much, so rather than have to list all the places to which he'd travelled to correct her misimpression of him, he decided to drop the subject.

"Justice, Alison's boyfriend, is in a band, so she likes travelling. We'll probably all be going on a lot of trips together," Sandra said, looking up from her phone. She turned from him to Stephanie, "When she's out with the drinks, tell Alison that Justice just told me he'll be here soon." She stood up and walked inside.

FOURTEEN

"Oh, no, I'm so sorry," she gasped.

Stephanie had spilled a glass of water on his book. He pulled it from the spill, and she started dabbing it with her paper napkin. She'd knocked the glass over with her elbow reaching for one of the shots that Lofton was carrying. "Don't worry about it," he said. By the looks of it, the damage was minimal, and in any case, as much as he loved books, he wasn't particularly conscientious about their physical upkeep. The book in question's cover was already torn, and it had its fair share of coffee stains.

"*The Idiot*," she remarked, reading the cover. Stephanie looked up, waiting for him to say more. Before he could, Alison interjected excitedly, "Yeah, Dostoevsky . . . "

Lofton, who had begun his own sentence nearly simultaneously as hers, pressed on without trailing off or pausing, "Oh! I love that book. We read *Crime and Punishment* in high school," he said.

Alison looked at him and smiled. "It happened again," he said, referring to the fact that everyone seemed to talk over her without noticing.

"What happened?" Sandra asked Alison puzzled. He could tell Alison was about to explain, but then she changed her mind. There was a silence.

"Well, before we get too far into books, first there's the shots," Lofton said. He lined them up.

"Lemon Drops," Alison said, peering over Lofton's shoulder as she looked at him.

"I already had a lemonade, too," he said.

"Can't have too much lemon," Stephanie laughed.

They lined up against the rail, the shot in their hands, counted to three, and swigged down the Lemon Drops. "Ahhh, just like candy," Lofton said.

He was about to turn to Stephanie and say something about the book, when Sandra said to her, "Seen any good movies lately?"

Stephanie's face lit up. "Bert and I have been watching a lot of movies. But for some reason I can't think of any right now," she laughed.

He generally didn't watch movies, but he did have a few he absolutely loved. He considered mentioning Terrence Malick, but decided instead to mention the Nicolas Winding Refn film that came to mind. "Do any of you like Refn?" No one but Lofton knew the director.

"Yeah, you ever seen *Bronson*?" Lofton asked.

"Yeah, really good, I thought. But you know, I think *Valhalla Rising* is good too," he said.

"Oh man, yeah. Great movie. People for some reason don't like it that much, but I don't get it," Lofton said.

Enthused that Lofton knew Refn, he mentioned the film he had in mind from the start. "Ever seen *Drive*?"

"Hah! 'Ever seen *Drive*?' Of course. Wanna watch it?"

"So you like it?" he asked.

"Yeah, man, I've watched that movie a thousand times. I was planning to watch it again soon, anyway. We should watch it tonight." Lofton paused for a moment and looked at Alison and the twins. "You're all invited of course," he said.

"Oh, thanks, but Bert and I were going to stay in tonight," Stephanie explained.

"Yeah, I'm going to pass too. Sounds fun, but I should probably get going," Sandra said.

Stephanie startled. "Wait, but I thought Justice was on his way?"

"No, he just texted me to say something's come up, so he won't be coming," she explained.

He looked over at Alison, whose hint of a smile suggested she may have had something to do with Justice's not coming by. She looked at Lofton. "I'll go," she said. "Never seen it."

"Well, then, great. How about you two come over at, say, seven-thirty?" Lofton assumed they were a couple, which was making Sandra uncomfortable.

"Sounds good," he said.

From his chair on the stairs, Rusty, who must have been listening to everything, said, "Good movie. You'll like it."

He turned to Alison. "Lofton lives just behind me, down the street. It's a short walk."

The sun was dropping below the Millrose Tower, and the same golden glow that had enveloped everything last evening was reemerging. Shooting up to the sky, the magnolia was shimmering in the golden rays, noble as always. He smiled at Alison and Lofton, happy with his earlier decision not to go off to the coffee shop. Enough arguing about squirrels, he thought.

FIFTEEN

AT the appointed time, Alison and he arrived, walking through the gates to The Oaks. The sky was streaked with turquoise plumes, which called to mind the days as a young boy when that had been among his favorite colors. Every day is a new day, he thought, another opportunity to work to begin again. There was no way to know what would come of his encounter with Alison. It was fragile, it was complicated, but he had an overriding sense of confidence, or better, of hope, that all would be well.

As they walked past the pool to Lofton's door and knocked, he looked at her, and she looked at him. They smiled and laughed, as she peeked through the blinds to see whether Lofton was coming to the door. She felt safe with him, and he felt at ease with her. Sometimes everything could feel easy, he thought.

The door opened, and Lofton waved them in with a smile. "Seven-thirty, exactly. Come on in, and make yourself comfortable," he said.

They had not brought any beer, and Lofton was not drunk. Lofton, who usually seemed deflated, at least at the bar, appeared a way that he'd never seen before, as if reinvigorated. He was pretty sure it was joy in Lofton, he saw.

"I don't have anything to drink," Lofton began to apologize.

"That's okay," Alison said.

"Well, let's put it on," Lofton said. He dimmed his living room's light, the screen came on, and the film began. They watched the opening shot, the hero, the Driver, standing alone in his Los Angeles apartment, staring out on the night skyline. The hero said into the phone,

There's a hundred thousand streets in the city. If I drive for you, you give me a time and a place, I give you a five minute window. Anything happens in that five minutes, then I'm yours, no matter what. Anything happens a minute either side of that, and you're on your own. Do you understand?

After what must be one of the greatest heist sequences in film history had concluded, the opening credits began rolling. Knowing the film like the back of his hand, Lofton snuck in a quick comment, turning his head to them from the other couch. "So awesome," he said, with a massive smile.

A second later, there was a jump cut to a stunning aerial night shot of the Los Angeles skyline, the roving view sonically accompanied by Kavinsky's anthem "Nightcall." In the room, listening to the song thumping, the three of them were translated into that mysterious space, in which it's impossible to differentiate the world of the film from the world of those watching it.

I'm giving you a night call to tell you how I feel.

The name of the lead actress flashed in pink cursive across the screen. Alison leaned over to him, and, cupping her hand over her mouth, whispered into his ear, "I don't like Carey Mulligan." Without saying a word, she put her head on his shoulder and clasped his hand.

The credits continued, the hero driving his car through the Los Angeles streets, a female voice singing over the song's electronic beat,

> There's something inside you
> It's hard to explain
> They're talking about you, boy
> But you're still the same.

The opening credits nearing their completion, the hero walked past the girl, she exiting their apartment building's elevator on her way to her car in the garage to work, the hero on his way up the elevator to his apartment. The elevator door closed as she walked away, and then a jump cut took them inside the Driver's apartment. While standing alone in his bedroom, the city lights shining in through the window, casting his shadow against the turquoise wall, the image of his double overlaying the cruciform shape of the window pane's shadow could be seen. That, he thought as he watched, was the entire movie condensed into one exquisite ten second symbolic sequence. It was a very simplistic story, of course. Good guy and girl fall in love. Good guy is tested by adversity, good guy overcomes evil in the name of love. Ultimately, love will require an act of sacrifice. The girl might never understand why he has done what he has, but he does it anyway, knowing it is what's best, no matter how hard it happens to be for him to do it. He smiled on the couch. If the others were watching with them now, they would be mocking what they saw: *cliché* and sentimental they would say. He was glad when she didn't say so. Instead, she squeezed his hand, and the opening credits ended.

When the movie was over, and they had left Lofton's, she to her house, and he to his, he lied in bed staring at the ceiling. He wondered whether she was at home, the same song from the movie stuck in her head that was now stuck in his.

> I don't sleep
> I do nothing but think of you
> I don't eat
> I don't sleep
> I do nothing but think of you
> You keep me under your spell
> You keep me under your spell
> You keep me under your spell
> You keep me under your spell
> You keep me under your spell
> You keep me under your spell.

He drifted into sleep, the expectation of tomorrow filling him with contentment. It meant one day closer to Saturday's party, when he would see her again.

Sixteen

Yesterday, which had been a Thursday, felt as if it belonged to another lifetime, for everything following on it was now unfurling in slow motion, the night when he had seen the movie with Alison itself feeling to have been an eternity ago, its resounding joy still resonating through the immediate surroundings of everywhere he found himself, since, unlike the past preceding that night, everything was now transformed and renewed, existence no longer laboring under the weight of what had been a familiar tedium and exhaustion. Being itself now was light, rendered translucent by the love he felt trembling forth from all things. Some of the changes were very small, yet no less profound. For example, although nobody he knew was sitting with him outside in the sun here at the coffee shop on Friday afternoon, this did not mean he was alone. He had Alison's number, which meant they were able to be in touch, and he was relieved to see that she was as eager to be texting about anything that came to her mind as he was to text her about what came to his. They shared mundane details about what they were doing during the day, and they swapped questions about everything, both serious and silly things. He could feel the transformation love was undertaking within him, hollowing out what had been there before, leaving nothing of the *I* in the wake of the *We* now crystallizing in its place.

He whittled away the afternoon hours, mulling over whether to ask her if she wanted to see him tonight. He decided against it for fear of appearing overeager. The evening came. He watched the sunset transfigure the clouds. God the artist, he thought. The clouds turned pink and orange, then purple, and then shifting shades of blue till night fell completely. On Fridays such as these, typically he would go out with friends to the bar, but when the sun began setting, he had finished his daily reading, closed out his tab, and went next door to the laundromat. He collected his clothes from the dryer, watched the sunset in solitude, and then said goodbye to Jackson and the others who were all showing up. He could see they wanted to ask why he wasn't staying for beer and dominoes, but nobody asked. He could tell they knew he wanted to be alone, not because he was depressed, but because he felt content, and didn't want to disturb the reverie of whatever it was they all saw was transforming him.

As he walked home, he hoped he might find Timothy in the courtyard, but his neighbor wasn't there. He went to Timothy's door and knocked. No answer. He gently pressed his ear to the door, and heard nothing. He considered asking others in the building if they had seen Timothy around, but nobody knew one another well enough for asking to do any good.

He made spaghetti. After dinner, he smoked cigarettes and read on the couch. Then, in order to hasten tomorrow, he went to bed early.

Saturday evening arrived. The party was set to begin at nine-thirty, but Jack had told him to come over earlier, if he wished. Some others would be there early too. He got there at eight. Jack and David's apartment lay on the second floor of a yellow brick house reminiscent of a charming East Coast home from a Hopper landscape. Tony, whom he had not seen since the lake outing, was pulling up to the front of the house. The Cuban waved through the windshield. Tony parked, popping his head of black hair above the roof, and pointed his thumb to the trunk.

"Hey man, I have some stuff in the trunk Jack asked me to buy. Think you could help me carry it in?"

He walked to the trunk. Tony opened it, and they grabbed some cases of beer.

"Tecate?"

Tony laughed. "Nasty, I know, but it's what he wanted."

There were two kegs to carry in also. As they approached the stairs, "You seem to be in a good mood," Tony said.

"Yeah, I met a girl."

"Oh, I see. Nice. What's her name?" They started up the stairs before he could answer.

They set the cases down on the floor of the living room, as David and Jack came in from the kitchen. "Tony!" David said ignoring him, "so good to see you."

"Thanks for bringing the beer up guys," Jack said looking at them both.

"No problem. There's more downstairs," he said.

The three of them went to the trunk, leaving David upstairs.

"These are pretty heavy. At the store, it took two guys to carry one," Tony explained. Jack and he lifted a keg together.

"Tell David to come down and help me with this last one," Tony said tapping on the other one. Reaching the top of the stairs with theirs, Jack and he were winded and sweating. Jack was coughing.

"I need a cigarette."

David laughed. "No, no you don't." Jack lit one anyway.

"Tony said to tell you he wanted you to give him a hand with the other one," he said to David.

He could see David thought he was inventing the request, as a way of distracting David from ridiculing Jack. Noticing David's incredulity, Jack chimed in to confirm the errand's authenticity. "If you don't want to do it, like Tony asked, that's fine. I can go down again, David," Jack said.

"No, no, it's fine." David laughed lightheartedly. "You can be such a baby sometimes, Jack."

A few minutes later, they had both kegs in the living room. "Okay, awesome. Now we just need to get them out to the yard," Jack observed.

Tony shook his head. "Yeah, you know, why didn't we just take them straight down the driveway to the yard?"

"I thought it might be nice to have them inside, but then I changed my mind. I think it'll be better to have them out in the yard. It's going to be nice tonight, so everyone will want to be outside, anyway," Jack said.

"Yeah right, Jack. Everyone knows you're a hypochondriac. There's no way to have a party at our place without having people inside. Face it, we invited too many people. But if you want the kegs in the yard, that's fine," David said.

Tony appeared to have found a solution. "Why not just have some-body else carry them down later?"

"Yeah, now there's a very good point. Let's have Brian do it," David concluded.

Tony's face was ashen. "Brian?" he murmured.

"Yes, Brian," David said, pretending not to understand why Tony would be alarmed.

Brian Hipple, a former art student from Boston, worked at one of the museums with a gallery installation team here in the city. His big auburn beard accentuated the roughneck impression and his place within the group as its self-styled Teddy Roosevelt, in short, the macho sophisticate. Brian was closest with Jack, although he was also on amicable terms with many of the others, including Clara, whom he'd briefly dated years ago before she'd met Paul. It made fine sense, then, that he'd be invited. The trouble was that Tony and Brian had been butting heads recently. About what exactly neither of them was able to say. Only a few weeks ago, while they were all drunk at the apartment one late night, Brian had threatened to throw Tony out the window or bash his head into the sink. No one, including Tony, could remember what had triggered the altercation. But in any case, everyone knew Brian had a long memory, was prone to grudges, and, given his size, he was not the type to be trifled with. If Brian was coming tonight, it might be to confront Tony again.

"Well, if Brian will be here, at least I came prepared," Tony smiled. He pulled a switch blade from his pocket and twirled it nonchalantly.

"Ah, great, now you're carrying a knife, so that when you pull it out, Brian can take it from you, and stab and kill you," David chortled.

Judging by the smile on his face, David was relishing the fact that he knew he was in fine form tonight. In order to keep the momentum going until everyone would be here, David would be throwing in the occasional jab at those around him, like a prize boxer sparring before he stepped into the ring. Early indications were that David's sarcasm was calibrated perfectly tonight, biting but not too acidic.

"Whatever, I'm ready," Tony said.

The witticisms and one-upmanship began in earnest. Rather than listen to the banter, he sat down on the couch in the conjoining room and thought about Alison.

"Hey, by the way, what about that girl you mentioned?" Tony asked after the banter subsided.

"Her name's Alison. She'll be coming, so you'll get to meet her," he said. He noticed something stirring within David, the Canadian's eyes dilating with a sense of possibility.

"It'll be good to meet her," Jack said. "Speaking of which, where is Mick?"

"He's not coming tonight," David said cryptically in a way meant to invite further questions. Everyone turned to David in surprise.

"Why not?" Tony asked.

"I don't know. He said he wants to be alone. He'd been counting on a number of academic job offers, but he wasn't interviewed. He thought he had a sure thing in Perth, some sort of postdoc, but that fell through unexpectedly on Monday, so now he has nothing. I saw him Tuesday on campus, drunk as a skunk. He even pissed on a tree." David shrugged.

"What's he going to do then?" Jack asked.

"He's not sure. Probably go back to Australia, maybe try the job market again next year," David said.

Tony turned to David. "Well, what about Cody?"

"He's with Paul and Clara right now. They said they'd be picking up beer when they finish dinner, so they should be here soon."

"Goat?" Tony asked.

David shook his head no. "Jessica."

Talk of Mick's academic woes triggered Tony to think of Karl. "What about Karl? Is he coming?"

"Nobody's heard from him. We tried calling him," David said glancing at Jack. Jack threw up his hands. "Sorry, no idea about Karl."

Without saying anything, everyone knew these absences marked an irreversible turning. For Mick and Karl to skip tonight's birthday party meant they both were tired of it all. They were reorienting themselves with an eye to a future that would no longer involve everyone here in the room. What that future would be was impossible to say, but the fact that everyone knew Mick and Karl were choosing the unknown over routine was impossible to ignore. There was no going back. After a long silence in which everyone recognized that all the times they had spent together were coming to an end, they accepted the reality of the newly contracted circle. The discussion turned to one of their favorite subjects, the terrible state of the academic job market. He wasn't interested in listening to everyone offer his theories about the causes for its ills and what should be done to fix them, so he went out to the landing on the back stairs, lit a cigarette, and texted Alison.

"Be there soon!" she said. He checked the time: nine o'clock.

Jack, whose dejection was growing the longer he thought about everyone who wouldn't be coming, leapt from the couch at the chance to answer the door, as somebody rung the bell. "Ah, I bet that's Cody and Clara," he said beaming, forgetting to mention Paul. Like everyone, Jack must have known that it was Paul who was still most tethered to routine, while Cody and Clara were far less so. Highlighting the fact that they were here, while pretending that Paul were an afterthought, was Jack's way of coping with the group's dissolution, and the undeniability of everything's fleetingness, above all his own life, this being something of a milestone for him, forty signifying the unambiguous end of his youth. Jack grabbed three Tecates from the table, and disappeared down the stairs.

"Hello," Clara could be heard saying in an excited voice when the door opened. "Happy birthday to the birthday boy!" she said.

"Hey, guys," he said. "Thanks so much for coming."

Jack walked in carrying a small gift box, Clara and Cody trailing behind him. They shut the door. Assuming he must be outside getting ready to bring something in, Tony turned to Clara, "Where's Paul? I can give him a hand."

Clara's cheeks flashed a red that matched her hair. She composed herself, and said casually, "Oh, Paul's not here. He decided to stay home tonight to get some work done. He's been working on a new collage."

Aside from the fact that everyone knew Paul had been looking forward to tonight's party, and that he could have picked another time to work, there was the fact that only a few hours ago, Paul had texted Jack and David to say he'd be picking up more beer for the party when he and Clara came over. But now Clara and Cody were empty-handed except for the gift, and Jack had not heard from Paul. He recognized the obvious, that Paul must have gotten too drunk to be able to come over, and Clara, worried that Uncle Paulie would rear its ugly head, had left him behind at their place. Cody, who had not said anything since arriving, appeared to be taking Paul's absence a little too nonchalantly. Judging by the way he was standing so closely to Clara, the chance to be here tonight without Paul was something he saw as a stroke of good fortune.

Having reached the same conclusion explaining Paul's absence, David turned immediately to practical matters. "Well, we're going to be short on beer. Cody, let's go down to the store."

David stood up, and walked out the door leading to the stairs, with Cody following him.

Tony shouted down the stairwell, "Hey, David, do you need the car?"

They heard a voice, its Canadian accent, echoing up to them, "No! We'll walk." The door knob turned and the front door shut.

A moment later there were footsteps coming up the stairs, with a number of loud voices and laughter. "Oh, others are here!" Jack rushed to the window overlooking the yard, stuck his face through the tattered blinds, and then walked through the living room to open the door.

"Happy birthday!" everyone shouted.

A group he had not met before walked into the living room carrying beer. A minute later there were more voices, as a couple walked in, and then another minute later there was more noise, as a trio of graduate students from Cody's philosophy program arrived. The floodgates had opened, and within half an hour the living room, dining room, and kitchen were full, with a dozen or so more people now gathering out in the yard. He was feeling a little hemmed in upstairs, so he decided to go outside. He walked down the stairs, and took a seat in the red gazebo underneath the tree. Jack had strung white lights over the gazebo and down the stairs. Someone was starting a fire in the pit. He thought about pulling up a chair at the fire, but instead he lit a cigarette, and watched the yard fill up. He knew most of the people there, some of whom would wave to him as they came in. Mostly, though, nobody seemed to notice his presence, which he liked.

By eleven, he was beginning to wonder where she was. He had drunk three beers while waiting, while making the rounds in the yard, greeting those he knew, and being introduced to people's friends and dates. There were too many names to remember. He scanned the yard, and didn't see her, so he decided to walk upstairs to see how Jack and Tony were doing.

Passing through the crowd in the kitchen, he was hardly able to hear anyone's voices over the sound of the music coming from the stereo at the top of the stairs. In the living room, he found Tony and Jack on the threshold to the dining room, greeting people as they showed up. He walked over. About to say something to them, the front door opened. Alison and a young man he'd never seen before came in. The man was tall and very handsome, with a slender build, and a chiseled face. The man looked unsure where to go when he entered, because the living space was already full. Alison grabbed his arm and pointed in the direction of where Tony and Jack were standing with him.

He waved to her, but she didn't wave, because she had a bottle of champagne with a ribbon tied around it.

"Hi," the man with Alison said, shaking Jack's hand. "You must be Jack."

"Yeah, dude. Very good to meet you," Jack said.

"I'm Preston," he said.

Realizing that Jack didn't recognize them, Tony offered his hand to Alison, "Can I help you take that?"

"Oh, yes, thanks. It's a gift," she said nervously without looking at Jack directly.

"Oh, wow, thank you, guys. Awesome," Jack said, taking the champagne.

"I'm Alison," she told them.

"Oh, I've heard about you from this guy," Tony said laughing, pointing at him.

He put out his hand to Preston, "Hi, good to meet you," he said.

As they were finishing with introductions, the door swung open. Cody and David were coming in, returning from another beer run at the corner store. Out of the corner of his eye, he noticed Clara, who had been sitting with some friends on the couch. Seeing them come into the room and anticipating that they would be walking over to Tony and Jack, she leapt up from the couch, heading to the group, since it would give her the chance to be nearer to Cody. More importantly, it would give her the chance to meet Alison.

"More beer! Great," she said to David and Cody, as she nuzzled up between Alison and Preston. She looked at Jack. "Champagne, Jack? Fancy too! Who brought that in here?" she laughed.

Jack looked at Clara, and then glanced to Alison. "Clara, this is Alison and—"

"Preston," the man said. He stuck his hand out to Clara, who shook it flirtatiously.

"Alison, is it?" Clara said.

"Yes."

"I'm Clara." She paused a moment. "Someone should help Jack with the champagne."

Tony grabbed the bottle from Jack. "Good idea. C'mon, let's go find a corkscrew."

Clara stared at him for a second, raising her eyebrows, and pointing with her eyes to Alison and Preston. Alison had come with somebody else in order to make him jealous, Clara seemed to be suggesting. Clara, of course, had her own self-serving reasons for wanting him to conclude so, but in any case, he didn't see it the way she did. Of course, he recognized that perhaps he was simply seeing what he wanted to see, but when he thought over his old friend's comments about how girls were always testing a man, he honestly did not see this as any kind of test. If it was one, it didn't bother him.

Cody leaned over to the table and grabbed a beer, handed one to Clara, and then turned pleasantly to Alison and Preston. "Guys?"

"Sure," Preston said flinching, clearly appalled at the prospect of drinking a Tecate.

"Alison?" Cody asked.

"No, thanks. I'll wait on the champagne."

The decision, which produced the social equivalent of a train derailment, upset everything. Preston felt like he'd taken a Tecate for no reason, and Cody's attempt at being friendly was quickly unmasked for what it was, a transparent ploy to tweak him by treating Preston and Alison as a couple. He could tell Alison already didn't like Cody. Cody, who was flushed with embarrassment having realized she was not stupid, and that his condescension had not gone unnoticed, fell silent. Even David was silent, unsure of what to say. Whatever his best laid plans for the night may have been, David was discombobulated by the fact that Alison had come with another man, and there was no easy way of reorganizing with another strategy after Cody had just blundered so clumsily right in front of everyone.

"I'll be back. Anyone want to go for a smoke?" Cody fumbled. David overcame the temptation to leave the embarrassing situation, the curiosity getting the better of him. "I'll smoke later," David said. No one else said anything.

Tony and Jack rejoined the group with glasses as Cody stepped aside, handing one to everyone in the group except for Preston, who was still holding his Tecate. Clara had chugged her Tecate already, and with her freshly freed hand, she grabbed a champagne glass. Preston stared at his beer with dread unable to find it within himself to finish. "Excuse me," he said, as he walked over to the line for the bathroom.

Alison walked over to stand next to him. "I did it," she smiled.

"What?" he asked.

"Justice. I broke up with Justice." Her face momentarily looked distant, and a sadness crept over it. She felt badly about hurting him.

He was ecstatic, but didn't want to gloat, especially since he understood Justice must be upset, so he asked gently, "How did he take it?"

"It was bad. I feel terrible, but I knew I had to do it. I can tell you later."

She slipped her hand into his, and they stood comfortably, a couple for everyone to see. Tony finished pouring the glasses, at which point he cleared his throat, tapped his glass, and waited till the upstairs fell quiet.

"I'll be brief," Tony began. "Thank you all for coming," he said, assuming a demeanor that made everyone in the room feel like they were back in the Old Country, their commanding but reassuring Cuban father issuing a word that would capture the mood everyone was feeling on the special occasion.

"As many of you know, I'm Tony. Jack and I have been friends for many years now. We were even roommates for a time, before he left me for David." The room laughed.

"He made the right choice," David interjected. The room laughed again.

"Anyway," Tony continued, "tomorrow Jack is forty. Or, I guess," he looked at a clock, "he's forty in ten minutes." Everyone burst out hollering and cheering and whistling. "Jack, happy birthday. And thank you to everyone for coming tonight. Enjoy your night, and let's have a toast to Jack!" Tony raised his glass to the ceiling. Jack sipped down his champagne, dabbed his chin, and shot a big grin to Tony—everyone cheered again.

"Hello. Welcome to our place," David said, outstretching his hand to Alison.

After the disaster with Cody, David was trying to disassociate himself from anything he knew she might suspect had been his doing. He could tell David was intrigued by her intelligence. David took on a bemused demeanor meant to suggest his surprise that she would be interested in the guy she was.

"Glad to see you dressed comfortably," he said, pointing to her ballet flats. She was in black jeans and a dark blue shirt. More strikingly, though, was the fact that she was wearing very little make-up, which was unique among the others at the party who had done themselves up more than usual. He knew David would find that intriguing as well. He could see David going through his internal check-list of admirable things he would like in a girl, or at least respect about someone's taste in one, and finding himself unable to find anything to dislike.

"You remind me of my ex-girlfriend," David said self-deprecatingly. Everyone laughed. It wouldn't take long before his clinical admiration for her personality turned into resentment that he didn't have somebody similar in his life.

Preston returned to the room, wincing when he saw Alison holding his hand. He looked like he was about to turn to the door, when Clara called him over to the group.

"Preston!" She had a way of using somebody's name she had just met to flatter, which in this case was effective, since the newcomer was understandably feeling adrift, alone at the party, with what he thought had been his date now holding another man's hand.

"Clara, is it?"

"Yes."

"Do we know each other?"

"I don't think so. We probably have mutual friends, though," she said. He could tell Preston wanted to say that was unlikely, but because he was in no position to insult anyone, seeing as he was so isolated, he nodded thoughtlessly instead. Cody walked into the room from having his cigarette, and, seeing Clara engaged with Preston, walked over to join the group. David was enjoying the desperation immensely.

"Preston, Cody is a philosophy student," David said. David was setting up a cock fight.

"I see," Preston said.

Noticing Preston looked unimpressed, Cody asked, "And what do you?"

Preston laughed nonchalantly, as if he were about to throw his arms over a recliner, and said, "Oh, nothing really. I'm an artist, or, well, I suppose more of a writer."

By this time souring on everything in her life, especially Paul at home, Clara had lost patience with the situation, and appeared ready to dispense pretending that she was seriously interested in Preston. That everyone was already feeling the effects of the champagne was a contributing factor.

"A writer?" she said dismissively. "What do you write?"

"Oh, things," he said vaguely, with an air of indifference.

"Well, tell us. It shouldn't be hard to explain," she asserted. David giggled. Jack lit a cigarette. Tony took a seat at the table. Cody put his hand to his chin, and stuck his lower lip out mockingly.

Sensing there was no way out, and that everyone wanted to hear an answer, Preston stammered, "Well, beauty. I'm writing about beauty. More specifically, about how our consumeristic age has commodified beauty in such a way that now what is actually ugly has come to be considered beautiful, and vice versa." It was amateur drivel, clearly, and David suppressed a laugh.

Looking at the others, David cracked, "I didn't know somebody invited Adorno."

There was no denying that David's joke was funny. But in a way, the joke made him sad. Sad for everyone. Sad for Preston, who was clearly uncomfortable. Sad for David, who enjoyed the satisfaction of putting Preston down. Then he felt badly about himself, when he realized how, on many occasions, he'd made jokes like this about others. He had been on the receiving end of many too. He thought about how everyone here gossiped about each other when he wasn't there, and he knew of course that he had been the subject of sustained ridicule and mockery when he wasn't there to hear it. And, of course, everyone knew the same was true of himself. For so long, the result had been a cynical sort of tacit agreement whereby everyone consented to be vicious to one another, for if anyone tried to object, it would be easy for whoever was being accused of cruelty to point out the hypocrisy, since invariably whoever was being attacked had at some point been the vicious one. Over the years, in this way, things had spiraled out of control, and it was difficult to imagine how the course could be reversed.

Sensing that Preston was being made fun of, Alison spoke up. "Preston isn't just a writer. He's also an artist. A very talented painter," she added.

Alison turned directly to Clara, who looked away.

"Sorry, what do you do, Alison?" Tony asked. "I should have asked earlier."

"I'm an art student," she said, too humble to say she was an artist. She said a few things about her charcoal drawings. Tony and Jack were impressed, Tony even at one point shooting him a "well done" look when she was talking. No longer being able to stand the envy welling up within, David waited for her to pause, then said, "I'm going to check on the fire downstairs," and walked out.

"He'll need my help," Cody said, following behind.

Clara stared at Alison and him. "It's crowded. Why don't we all go downstairs also?"

They walked through the kitchen. When they went out the door to the landing, Alison squeezed his hand, and told him to stop. They stood there, taking in the sight of the white lights, the fire, and the crowd of people smoking and drinking and talking. The moon was full. "Look at that," she said. Without saying a word to her, or she to him, they knew to make their way to the red gazebo.

They passed through the crowd of others, taking the seat another couple had just left. When they sat down, they kissed. She laughed, and they kissed again. They sat in silence for a few minutes, sipping their champagne, watching the yard. She stood up. "I'll be right back."

She weaved across the yard through the crowd. A Modest Mouse song, "Never Ending Math Equation," began playing. He looked to the stereo to see Jack had put on the song. He was going to smile, but Jack by then was feeling the effects of the champagne and Tecate, and was too drunk to notice.

Watching Jack and everyone else there, he understood that even if the universe did work on a math equation, that had nothing to do with existence, since existence was human, full of hopes, and dreams, and desires, and thoughts, and regrets, and so many other things, none of which had absolutely anything to do with what a math equation could ever say about it at all. Even Jack, who in the heat of a philosophical debate was prone to be the one to argue that the universe was inherently mathematical, did not truly believe it, he could now see plainly. Here Jack was drunk on his fortieth birthday, and the last thing on his mind was a math equation. He saw Jack had put the song on, probably because he liked that line, but it was a line that was impossible for him to live by, something that had no real bearing on where Jack, and everyone else there, found themselves.

He watched Alison exit the crowd on the driveway, where she found Preston waiting. He was still alone, and he looked resigned. She walked up to him. They said a few words to one another, and he leaned down to hug her. They embraced for a few seconds, and then he turned around, vanishing into the night.

He glanced over at Jack again, who was now standing in the yard with Tony, David, Cody, and Clara. Clara, he saw, had watched Alison and Preston hug goodbye. He could see Clara scanning the crowd, looking to find him. Her eyes finally reached the gazebo, where she saw that he had seen her tracking Alison. She glanced away embarrassedly.

Alison, who was worried he would be jealous, threw on a big smile as she walked back, locking eyes with him the entire way over to the gazebo. She sat down next to him, put her hand on his knee, and rested her head on his shoulder.

Later that night, when the party was over and all the guests had left, they sat alone in the gazebo talking. He hadn't been planning on it, but they had sex. When they were finished, and they were about to leave, she said, "Oh, no, my purse! I left it upstairs." They looked up at the second story. The lights were off.

"C'mon, let's go," he said, leading her up the stairs. They reached the door, and turned the knob. It was locked.

"Let's try the front door," she said.

"It'll be locked. Jack and David live upstairs anyway, and their downstairs neighbor is home. He went to bed a long time ago, so we can't knock."

She was staring at the windows, looking to see whether there was a way to climb inside. He knocked on the door a few more times. Still no answer. Then he had an idea. He walked to the railing, leaned over, and gently tapped the window.

"What's that?" she asked.

"David's room," he whispered.

"Isn't he asleep?"

"Maybe. The light went off a few minutes ago. He might still be awake."

She looked at him knowingly. It was a longshot that he would let them in. She knew David and he had a contentious relationship, so she was not expecting anything. Just as they were about to lose hope, the door opened.

"Come on in you idiots," David said in his night robe. It was dark, but he could almost see David crack a smile.

SEVENTEEN

THEY slept late together, tired from last night. They didn't know what else to do, but because they didn't want to stay cooped inside the apartment on such a sunny afternoon, they decided they would stop by the bar. Lofton might be there.

It was more crowded inside than they had expected. They grabbed the last pair of stools at the counter, the same spot, they both realized, as the one the night they met. Billy came over. "What'll it be?"

"Two Lone Stars, please," he said.

An older man who was sitting alone stirred. "Always a fine choice," the man said.

The man looked to be in his early fifties, his matted gray hair reaching down to his glasses. He was wearing a leather jacket, which he removed and placed on the counter beside his whiskey glass.

"Come here often?" the man asked.

He hesitated, embarrassed to admit that he did. The man laughed. "I understand," he said.

"I'm Alison." He gave his name too.

"Very nice to meet you both. I'm—" a loud honk from a car made his name inaudible. He thought about asking the man to say his name again, but by the looks of it, the man was not planning to leave any time soon, so there would be time to ask later.

"You two from around here?"

"She is," he said pointing to Alison.

"Is that so?" the man said.

"Yeah. I like it. But we might be moving. Or, well, he might be," she said.

"Moving?" the man asked.

"Yeah. We'll see," he said.

"To where?"

"Oxford."

"Oxford! Wow, very impressive. What for?"

"Philosophy," he answered.

"Philosophy! Wow, very, very impressive." The man shot a glance at Alison with a good-natured smile, and said, "You might want to hang on to this one."

She laughed, "I know."

The man gestured outside, "Well, as for me, I'm just passing through."

Alison was curious. "You're not from here?"

"Me? Oh, no, I'm not from here." He smiled. "I'm a pilot."

"A pilot? Very cool," he said.

"Yeah, well, I'm in town for a safety re-certification program. They bring us in, so I'll be here for the next few days, before I head home to Florida."

The man didn't say anything more about the program. He thought about asking whether the program was strictly a matter of written examinations, or whether there was any actual flying involved. He didn't say so, but there was an irony in a pilot drinking before he was going to be flying as part of a safety certification. He decided not to ask. Sometimes it was better not to question somebody, when doing so would lead the person to lie, he decided.

The man looked on them with a warm approving smile. Rather than embittering him, the sight of their youth seemed to be uplifting him. "Boy, I'll tell you what, you two are in love," he chuckled. He paused. Then he stared right at them, and without a trace of hesitation said, "You two should get married."

There was nothing jocular about the statement. The man said it with seriousness, as someone who had seen many couples over the years, as someone who maybe had been married himself once.

"Maybe one day," he said to the man.

"Maybe one day?" the man chuckled. "Look at this young lady. She's beautiful, and she's in love with you. Tell him, sweetie, you are in love with him, aren't you?"

They sat in silence, with Alison blushing. "Well, see, there you go. You two don't say anything to each other, but it's pretty darn obvious to me from where I'm sitting," the man laughed. "You don't know what you'll have tomorrow," he said, taking a sip of his whiskey. "If you love each other, you should say it, and you should get married."

That evening when they were walking home from the bar, he realized he had not asked for the man's name. He would simply remember him as The Pilot.

They entered the apartment. He sat on the couch, and she stood in the bedroom doorway. He stood up, and they stared at each other.

"So, are you going to marry me or what?"

She laughed, pretending he was joking. He was silent.

"Are you serious?"

He was silent still.

"You big dummy, you don't even have a ring! That's not how you ask someone to marry you!" she laughed. He could tell that she had just said yes.

"Yes, I'll marry you."

EIGHTEEN

I F the days immediately following their date at Lofton's had left time dilated, the elongation between when he had seen her last and when he would see her again languishing on like an eternity, now that they were engaged, and saw each other every day, things felt like one continuous day, an endless moment for which there was nothing otherwise to be desired. It had been three months, and here in the first weeks of fall, her family was to leave for a short trip to the Pacific Northwest. She would leave Thursday and return Monday, only to be gone then for a long weekend.

He had seen very little of everyone else since Jack's birthday party. On Friday night, however, he was on his couch reading, when Tony unexpectedly called to invite him to a party at a place near Paul and Clara's. He agreed to go, and Tony said he'd be by his place at ten to give him a ride there. A few minutes before Tony's arrival, he went out to the courtyard for a cigarette. The three women who'd been drinking their iced teas last summer were at the same table, once again drinking their iced teas.

"Hi, guys," he said. He lit a cigarette.

"Want some tea?" one of them asked. She was an older woman in her fifties, with gray hair, and big kind blue eyes. Evidently her son, whom she once had said reminded her of him, was coming tomorrow for a visit from out of state. She told him more about her family, and the group exchanged family stories. As he was about to sit down and have a glass of tea, he heard Tony's car pull up. The Cuban rolled the window down, "Ready when you are."

"Have you seen Timothy?" he asked the women.

"Is that the young man we see you with sometimes, the one who also lives in the building?" a second woman asked.

"Yeah, the one with blond hair," he said.

"Oh, yes, I know who he is," she said. "I haven't seen him around in a long time." Turning to the other two, she asked, "Have you?"

The woman whose son was coming to visit said, "No, haven't seen him." She looked like she wanted to say something else, but didn't. "We'll be praying for him," she said.

He stood up, gesturing to Tony. "Well, I have to be going."

The three women nodded politely and smiled. "Have a good night, sweetie, emphasis on good," the third woman who had not yet spoken anything said. He was about to say that he would, but he fell silent.

"Thanks."

The party was at the house of two baristas who worked at the coffee shop. Many people he recognized from the shop were there, as well as a number of others that had been at Jack's party. Loud electronic music was playing inside, along with flashing disco lights. Everyone had glowsticks wrapped around their necks. A girl with glitter on her face came outside and put one around his neck. He wanted to take it off, but he kept it on, just not to be rude.

"Oh, awesome, I love rave parties," Tony said. "Makes me miss Miami."

Seeing he wasn't in the mood to go inside, Tony offered to grab him a beer. "I'll be right back," Tony said. A few minutes later, he came onto the front porch with Cody following behind him.

"Look who I found inside!" Tony said smiling.

"Hi, Cody," he said.

"Hey."

There were a few seats on the porch, but they decided to stand. They watched the cars drive by for a while in silence.

Tony turned to Cody.

"So, any news, man?"

Cody shook his head. "No, not yet. Notifications should be coming out any day, though. Garson says things are extremely competitive, but he's confident I'll have a few good options. Rutgers, MIT, Wisconsin, Pittsburgh—I think Pittsburgh would be great." The fact Cody mentioned only the top philosophy of science programs in the country suggested he was still feeling optimistic about his admissions chances.

"Great, man. Keep me posted," Tony said.

Cody stared into the street. "You guys hear the news about Paul and Clara?"

"No," said Tony.

"They broke up yesterday. Clara told me," Cody said smiling.

"Yeah, well, I suppose we all saw that one coming," Tony said.

There was another long silence, after which they began discussing the relationship between the philosophy of science and metaethics. From what he knew about Cody's interests, he anticipated it wouldn't be long before Cody took the conversation as an opportunity to lay out his views about what sort of error theory would be needed in order to account for our everyday ethical discourse.

"You know, when I first delved into this issue in my first year in the program," Cody said, "I was only interested in problems within the philosophy of science. But as I learn more, and read more, I really think there's a need to reform metaethics in light of what's really going on in the philosophy of science. There are non-realists about value who have various naturalistic arguments, but they are ignorant of the actual science, and the developments in the philosophy of science, which I think is a huge problem." Without meaning to do so, he sighed at Cody's comment. Cody shot him a glare.

"I'll be back. Excuse me," he said to Tony and Cody.

He walked inside and made his way to the kitchen where he knew there would be beer. It was dark and crowded. Everyone was in the other rooms dancing, which left the kitchen empty. He made out the silhouette of a Lone Star pack on the counter near the refrigerator, grabbed four of them, sighed again, and thought how he was glad that he no longer felt enthusiasm for being at places like these. He vowed that if Cody had not yet stopped talking about atoms and the void when he returned to the porch, he would not lose his patience. It wasn't worth arguing.

He walked onto the porch. Cody and Tony were in the same spot, Cody waving his cigarette wildly to emphasize whatever point was at issue, as Tony was laughing.

"No, no. That's the entire mistake! When you realize that our everyday ontologies carve reality up in a way that is completely detached from the world, then you realize all of our everyday statements, not just our everyday moral statements, stand no chance of being true, because they don't refer to any states of affairs in the world." Tony and Cody grabbed the beers he offered them without looking at him.

"Okay, that's basically what Russell said. Or the point Wittgenstein later made against his earlier self," Tony said.

He decided to interject. "If everything's an illusion, then isn't your theory too?"

Cody smirked. "I'm not sure what you mean."

"Well, excuse me if I'm wrong. I missed some of what you've said while I was inside, but from what I gather just now, you think the everyday world, what someone like Flanagan or others call the manifest image of reality, is in fact an illusion, whereas the scientific image, whatever that precisely consists in, is true reality. Right?"

"I don't know if I agree with everything about Flanagan's characterization of the manifest image. I'm more interested in Nelson Goodman."

"The point is that things we take for granted, such as free will, value, and morality, those things, you believe to be illusory. But then so is your scientific theory about them."

"Well, it depends on what you mean by free will. I certainly reject libertarian free will. But there are compatibilist versions worth considering."

"Setting compatibilism to the side, you yourself are a hard determinist."

"Of course. Agent causation is conceptually incoherent, and even if it weren't, there's absolutely no empirical evidence for its existence, anyway."

"I don't know if it's incoherent. Kant didn't think it was. In any case, I don't think there's much scientific evidence in support of the idea free will is illusory. People always say that there is, but that's actually just a perfect example of what Heidegger would call *Gerede*."

The reference to Heidegger, whom Cody had never read, ruffled his feathers.

"You don't know the scientific literature. The studies are conclusive, or at least overwhelming," Cody countered.

"How do you know?" he asked. Cody assumed he meant to ask how many studies Cody himself had read, or how many such studies exist, or how persuasive they are. But he meant something else. He was pointing to the absurdity of proceeding as if knowledge itself were even possible if the scientistic paradigm Cody was defending were true.

"The only way anyone could know anything of that sort, especially on a broadly empiricist view, which is ultimately the one you're committed to, is through the senses. You have to perceive such things. The scientist uses his vision to walk into the lab, uses his touch to manipulate his instruments, his hearing to listen to others, and so on. It would not be possible to even conduct a scientific experiment designed to call into question the validity of the manifest image without depending on the life-world. Even the scientist who thinks it's an illusion, lives in it."

"Okay, so you're making a basic self-refutation argument. You're saying that if the naturalistic theory of knowledge and experience were true, then it would have to be false, since it would only undermine itself. I don't know why you're making this argument. There are already responses to those sorts of arguments in the literature. Philosophers of science and naturalists have ways of responding."

"In ethics?"

"Of course. That's what Tony and I are talking about."

"So, you think there aren't moral truths?"

Tony interrupted, "Yes, I think that myself. I'm not sure what Cody thinks."

"I agree with Tony. Moral propositions are useful fictions that have pragmatic value. That's it."

"Pragmatic value? You're detached from reality. It's scary. You think you're getting closer to truth with your theories, but the deeper you get into them, the less you understand anything at all, especially what's closest to you."

Cody sighed, and smiled smugly. "People just don't like to accept the truth that the universe isn't structured the way that we experience it. Humans are anthropomorphic." The view of the clouds on the drive out to the lake came to mind, as he thought about how that word—anthropomorphism—always did so much work for those who use it.

He watched the others on the porch, all of whom were oblivious to the three of them. People at a party immersed in their own lives as much as they were their own, people with no idea about what they were discussing. He looked onto the street, saw the cars, and lit another cigarette.

"So would it be an illusion, then, if one of these girls killed her friends here at the party, and we all decided that her doing so had been wrong?"

"I told you. Society needs order. If she were to do that, she should be arrested and punished," Tony said.

"Yeah, don't be stupid. I hate when you do this. You're smart. You're caricaturing the view. There's nothing about moral nihilism that entails retributive attitudes have no place in society. Though one day, our legal and others societal systems will be reformed in light of what the science teaches us," Cody said.

"You mean, when it tells us that nobody is free, so nobody's responsible for anything," he said.

"That's an oversimplification," Cody said.

"Is it? You're the one who just said that if that girl over here shoots that other girl over there here at this party, anyone who thinks it was wrong is being taken in by an illusion."

"That doesn't mean people won't react by treating it as wrong."

"But I'm not making a point about how people will or won't react. I'm making a point about how they ought to react. Or not just that. I'm saying they ought to react by judging it's wrong, because it is wrong."

"Fine. What makes it wrong?"

"You tell me why it isn't wrong. I don't need a theory of everything to know it's wrong for that girl here to shoot that girl there here on this porch right now. I can see that it is. But you're the one saying otherwise, so you're the one who needs the theory. You were saying a few minutes ago to Tony that you were going to be working on that question in graduate school, so what's the theory? I told you why I think that any such theory, which claims everyday reality is an illusion, is itself the illusion. It's clear to me if she shot her," he said gesturing to the girls sitting on the porch, "that is wrong."

There was a silence. He said, "What's the old Nietzsche quotation from *Beyond Good and Evil* about interpretation—"

Tony interrupted, "'There are no moral phenomena at all, but only a moral interpretation of phenomena.'"

"Yes, that's the one. In the same text, Nietzsche also says, 'Physics is only an interpretation and exegesis of the world (to suit us) and not a world-explanation.' So on Nietzsche's view, you two are selectively choosing which interpretations of the world you want to believe are more than illusion. That was my original point. I don't see how Cody can consistently deny the reality of morality in the way he does, while simultaneously appealing to science, as if it tells us how the world really is."

"So, now you're using a G.E. Moore style argument here," Tony said.

"I don't know, maybe. That's not the point. Attribute the argument to whomever you want."

"People would judge that the act of killing was wrong, but ultimately it isn't," Cody said, his eyes flashing with venom.

"Okay, what if one of the girls came over right now as we're standing here and shot Tony?" They saw where the line of questioning was going, but they had decided to accept the conclusions, no matter how preposterous.

"Same thing," Cody said. Tony nodded in agreement. "I can't be biased, just because it's me."

"Okay, what if she came over here and killed both of you?"

"No difference. Still not wrong," Cody said.

"Okay, what if she came over here and killed all three of us?"

"It's not wrong. Don't you get it? How many times do we have to tell you?"

"So, killing us all so that we couldn't be having this conversation right now, isn't wrong?" They looked at him silently. "Then how does this conversation even matter, if it matters so little that the girl over there could come over and kill us, and that wouldn't make it wrong?"

"You're making an appeal to emotions," Tony said. "All that matters is what's rational."

"You think it's rational to believe it's okay for someone over there to kill everyone at this party? How is that rational?"

"Because what we now know about the cosmos shows that there just aren't moral facts or truths. People don't want to believe it, and maybe society needs to believe there are such truths for the purposes of utility, but the arguments show otherwise."

"Okay. Then go over right now and tell them what we've been talking about. Tell them that their lives don't matter, because if Tony pulled out a gun and shot them dead, that wouldn't really matter, because everything's atoms and the void, and that Tony wasn't free anyway because determinism's the case, and if anyone thinks otherwise, they're the victim of an anthropomorphistic illusion. Go ahead," he said gesturing to the girls. By now, the girls were looking over and smiling at them.

"Just because I'm not going to do that doesn't mean anything. It doesn't change the truth," Tony said.

"You're right, Tony. It doesn't mean anything. You could just as well be Norman Bates, and it wouldn't matter. That's your view about everything, anyway."

"That's an equivocation on the term 'mean anything' and you know it! When I say that it wouldn't mean anything for me to tell those girls that it's not wrong to shoot them, that doesn't mean that I'm committed to holding that nothing matters."

He shook his head and began laughing at the ridiculousness of the words coming out of Tony's mouth. Even Tony was smiling. He could see Tony was seeing his point, even if he would not say so.

He continued. "I mean, if this is what you guys truly believe, then why do anything at all? After all, that question doesn't make sense on your view, since if you're right, there's nothing you can do anyway about it, since everything simply happens as it does, including whatever you do or don't do. Shoot those girls, and it does not matter; do not shoot the girls, and it does not matter; the girls shoot us, and it does not matter, the girls don't shoot us, and it does not matter. Nothing matters."

In a way he had not felt before, Tony was seeing the theory he had been endorsing had the bizarre feature of making absolutely no practical difference whatsoever to how he actually experienced the world or what he did in it. It was something he would think about periodically, for example in a philosophy class when he was teaching it to students, or like here, when he was arguing drunkenly among friends. But it was simply a notion to him, some words on a page or on the blackboard, the equivalent to a little toy on a shelf that he would occasionally take into his hand and inspect for his amusement before putting it away again.

With Cody, it was very different. And he could see that Tony saw the difference also. Cody was trying to somehow live out the belief that everything was an illusion, that nothing mattered. A twisted smile came across Cody's face. He was taking pride in the fact that they both could see he relished the belief that everything was meaningless.

The disguise was off, and Cody knew it. The young philosopher of science was training himself in the cult of nothing. What that could entail got the imagination to run wild, since the idea of somebody living in a way that had truly internalized what it meant to exist in a universe where nobody was free, and nobody was responsible, and nobody mattered, was frightening. A powerful wind began blowing, hissing through the power lines. Even though he was the type to tell himself it was a pure coincidence, it was enough to unsettle Tony. Out here on the dark porch, the conversation had shown Tony something that Tony had not wanted to see in Cody. Cody, for his part, was glad that Tony now did. He called to mind the time last year when everyone had been at one of the bars and Clara had pointed to him and Cody: "Ya'll got some weird White Spy and Black Spy thing going on between you two."

Standing here on the porch, he knew Tony recalled that moment also. At the time, Tony hadn't understood what Clara had seen. Now, however, Tony was beginning to understand. "I'm getting tired, and this party sucks.

I think I'm going home," Tony said. He turned from Cody and looked at him. "You need a ride?"

They left the porch, dodged some fallen tree branches, and got in the car. As they drove away, Cody was gone, having already disappeared into the blacklight party.

NINETEEN

THE sun was out on Tuesday. There was a knock on his door. He opened it to find Alison standing in a sundress and sunglasses. She threw her arms around him. "I missed you!" she said.

"I missed you too," he said, even if he was embarrassed to admit it, since he wanted to look tougher than he really was. They had plans to meet the twins at the bar for an afternoon drink. The engagement had come as a surprise to everyone they knew, and now everyone was trying to meet the couple.

"Mind if I leave my things here on the couch?"

"Not at all," he said. They laughed together when they both realized that of course she could, since they were engaged now.

They stepped into the sun, and took the usual path he always took, the one that led through the park with its fountain and magnolia.

"How was the trip?"

"I'm so glad it's over. I can't stand trips with my family. By the end of it, I'm always exhausted."

He was about to ask why, when they stopped at the scene before them. A crowd of people were standing outside the bar, with policemen pushing them off the steps, and rolling out caution tape. An ambulance was parked out front with paramedics inside. They saw people crying.

"Everyone, step back. Step back, please. Please, everyone, show some respect," a police officer said.

A young man standing beside them turned to his friends, "What's going on?"

"I heard somebody got shot," one of them said.

"What?"

"Yeah, just a few minutes ago."

"What happened?"

"Greg and Melanie were inside. They're talking to the cops now at the station. They said some guys came in, trying to rob the safe in the back, and somebody tried to stop them. He got shot. Some crazy Bonnie and Clyde stuff."

"Who got shot?"

Just then, they saw Lofton, who had been standing nearby. Lofton turned to everyone. "It was a guy who works the door," he said softly. Lofton looked at Alison and him, then looked away.

They pushed their way to the front, where they saw Billy in tears.

"What happened?"

"Rusty's dead."

For perhaps the first time since moving here, he was willing to see the place before him for what it is, for what it had always been, starting with the structure itself. Truth be told, it was little more than a dilapidated residential home that no family would understandably want, its chipping beige paint, rusting sheet metal roof, and rickety stairs, all making for an advanced decrepitude that stringing some tacky white lights stood no hope of mending. This physical dilapidation suited it, above all, because the bar, when considered not merely as a building, but as a place possessed of a character, was frankly worse than dilapidated, but rather outright depraved. The only thing more tattered than the floor's stained and frayed carpets were the sullied and battered hearts of those who, unable to leave as if under its spell, clung to the illusion that kept them there, to the collective delusion that if everyone continued straining to stay in the thinnest of bare moments, the despondence pervading the place, as well as those within it, would be dispelled. He looked at the place, which he saw was a house of horrors, mortified that it had ever exercised the hold over him that it had, and for so long. He looked sorrowfully over at Alison, who was staring numbly, the same painful lucidity seeping into her as well.

Without having to say a word, they left. When they got in the apartment, the twins began calling and texting Alison, but she didn't answer. She crawled into bed. He stood in the room and looked at her. He stared at her for a long time, trying to decide what he should say. Eventually, he felt like telling her not to worry, that Rusty was with Christ now. But he knew she wouldn't believe him, and in any case, she herself didn't know if she believed in heaven anyway. She looked up from the pillow, her eyes swollen shut with tears.

"Why would anybody do that? It's not fair," she sobbed.

He thought about telling her there wasn't anything more to say other than that what happened was wrong. But he knew she already knew.

TWENTY

A WEEK later, the shock was subsiding, and life was beginning to return to normal. The robbers had been apprehended at a gas station in Louisiana, evidently on their way to New Orleans. They would be returned to Texas to stand trial. It occurred to him how one day they probably would be executed in Huntsville. He imagined how someone might visit the museum and read an account of the murderers and Rusty, and yet still not have the slightest clue about what had really happened, or what it really meant. He tried to think what he would say if somebody asked him to explain, to articulate exactly what he had in mind when he felt that the museum would never be able to capture what happened, but he gave up trying to find the words, when he realized he never would.

He had returned home to California for a visit. He had hoped to introduce his parents to Alison, but that would have to come later. She was on another short trip with her family, this time to Tucson to see her uncle, so it would be a few weeks before the two families met.

He was studying the oak trees on the hillside when his mother called to him. "There's a letter for you, sweetie," she said, standing by the mail box.

He strode over, and grabbed it. "Thanks," he said.

She looked nervous. It was an envelope with a royal airmail sticker and an Oxford return address. For important mail, he always used their address, so that no matter where he happened to have moved, it would eventually find him.

"I'll go inside," she said.

He took a deep breath, opened the letter, and looked for the essential,

I am delighted to inform you that your application for admission to the University of Oxford as a graduate student has been successful. We would like to offer you a place for the DPhil in Philosophy beginning . . .

The first thing to do would be to call Alison with the news.

The oaks were swaying in the wind. He thought about how if he were writing a story, or even just keeping a diary, it would be possible to convey things in a few deceptively simple statements. It would be possible to condense a complicated series of everyday events, or better, the momentary intersection of many lives that had been their common existence, into a few sentences. Of course, there was something about the truth that would never be fully understood by anyone who had not experienced it directly. And even for those who had, still not everything would be entirely comprehensible. A summary was capable of imparting a degree of what had transpired, if not what it all meant.

He contemplated what he might say if he tried. He started with what he thought was most obvious. He would go to Oxford, and be Alison's husband. Mick, humbled for now, would one day succumb again to hubris, circumstances permitting. Having left for home in Alberta, David would finish his thesis on Buber, and then claw his way into an academic post he would resent. Jack, who had no plans to leave the city, would hang on to his beer and cigarettes for as long as he could, until finally his health gave out. Karl would disappear, probably to Austin. Tony would return to Miami to build a family of his own, his beliefs about atoms and the void forever remaining relegated to the classroom only. Cody, who had not received an acceptance to a doctoral program, would try reinventing himself as something else, his hope of becoming a great philosopher left by the wayside. Paul, who would never stop missing Clara, would cozy up to Jack, the two united in their shared commitment to staying when everyone else was leaving. Clara would soon leave as well, to where exactly, even she didn't know. Carrell would move into his mansion, seeking disciples, squashing anyone who had other intentions. Justice, who had the money, would leave for Europe, and maybe even walk among the birds on the Seine. Timothy might well end up in an institution, if not under a bridge.

It wasn't the blind necessity of fate. Nor was it chaos. People scoff, he knew, but it was Providence, the result of each person's decision to cooperate with, or else resist, the hand of God in his individual life. This wasn't the best of all possible worlds. But it was a world that stood redeemed, and that was good enough. He stopped thinking and paused. It lasted only a moment. And yet what the flicker of intuition revealed could not be denied. No matter what others said otherwise, he saw. Things were more than an exodus to nowhere.

www.ingramcontent.com/pod-product-compliance
Lightning Source LLC
Chambersburg PA
CBHW060810250626
47162CB00005B/1735